# EL CAPITAN'S ENEMIES

Outnumbered was putting it mildly. The two battle-hardened Texans, a dispirited gunsmith and three small-time felons fled the Rodriguez calaboose and joined forces with a vengeance-hungry Arkansas sodbuster to unite in a common cause — to rid the southwest of the murderous band led by a megalomaniac. The enemy was formidable, seemingly invincible. And still the challengers kept up the pursuit, all the way into Mexico for a fight to the finish.

# MARSHALL GROVER

◆

# EL CAPITAN'S ENEMIES

## A Larry & Stretch Western

*Complete and Unabridged*

# LINFORD
*Leicester*

First published in Australia in 1980 by
Horwitz Grahame Pty Limited
Australia

First Linford Edition
published 1998
by arrangement with
Horwitz Publications Pty Limited
Australia

British Library CIP Data

Grover, Marshall
  Larry & Stretch: El Capitan's enemies.
  —Large print ed.—
  Linford western library
  1. Western stories
  2. Large type books
  I. Title
  823 [F]

  ISBN 0–7089–5364–6

Published by
F. A. Thorpe (Publishing) Ltd.
Anstey, Leicestershire

Set by Words & Graphics Ltd.
Anstey, Leicestershire
Printed and bound in Great Britain by
T. J. International Ltd., Padstow, Cornwall

This book is printed on acid-free paper

# Author's Foreword

*The intrusion of a company of U.S. cavalry into Mexican territory, undoubtedly a breach of international law, might have triggered an official protest from the Mexican government were it not for the unusual circumstances prevailing at the time, midsummer of 1880.*

*President Rutherford B. Hayes received no complaint from his Mexican counterpart. The incident was forgotten, rating no mention in the files of the State Department in Washington. Obviously all parties concerned were reluctant to pursue the matter.*

*Heads of government, it must be conceded, can be discreet when it suits their purpose. Not so discreet, forever willing to trespass on foreign soil to do battle with a common enemy, were the two roughneck Texans who led that violent escapade.*

*Needless to report, their names were Lawrence Valentine and Woodville Emerson, better known as Larry and Stretch.*

# 1

## Reprisal in Sonora

'What the hell . . . ?' The taller Texan came awake with a start, eyes widening incredulously. 'Damn it, runt, we said Inagua is the most peacable little town we ever found . . . '

'And now — it sounds like all hell's bustin' loose,' growled his partner. Larry Valentine rolled off his bed and got to his feet. 'And I smell somethin' burnin'.'

' 'Less we hustle, it could be *us* burnin',' fretted Stretch Emerson.

After crossing the Arizona-Mexican border, the trouble-prone strangers had traveled 24 hours through Sonora to find what appeared to be the ideal resting place for a couple of knights-errant seeking elusive respite. Inagua was nought but some three dozen buildings clustered together on the alkali flats. A few of the buildings were of frame and clapboard, most were adobes. The Texans immediately caught the atmosphere of this out-of-the way retreat, admiring the lethargy of the locals. Lethargy was what they needed, they assured themselves. A belly-full of Mexican food, a couple of soft beds, a place to stable their horses; their needs were simple.

They had arrived in the hour before noon, had eaten their fill of chili-con-carne at fat Bernadino's cantina and accepted Bernadino's offer of the use of a double bedroom upstairs. From around 12.15 p.m. they had slept. Now they were wide awake, smelling smoke and hearing the grim sounds of turmoil, a thunder of gunshots, the screams of terrified women and children, the cries of the injured. This peaceful Mexican village was under attack — obviously.

It was a rear room and the doorway was obscured by darting flames and weaving smoke when, having hastily

2

donned their clothes and strapped on their Colts, the Texans grabbed saddle-bags rifles and packrolls and hustled to the open window. Their gear was dropped into a back alley. They followed it, hanging from the window-ledge, then letting go, falling with legs slightly bent. Larry flopped sideways after hitting ground. Stretch pitched forward on face and hands, but was quickly on his feet and emptying his holsters. Being ambidexterous with handguns, he packed twice as much .45 as his partner, the holsters slung to either hip from a buscadero-style cartridge-belt.

The alley was almost completely obscured by dust and smoke. They glimpsed their pudgy host huddled by a trash-heap on the other side of the alley, watching through dilated, despairing eyes as his cantina burned. Their first thought was for their horses. Having satisfied themselves Bernadino had gotten clear, they began stumbling in the general direction of the barn where they had stabled Larry's sorrel and Stretch's pinto.

What they saw when a gust of wind dispelled dust and smoke from the area to their right started their scalps crawling. A woman lay in the dust some 20 yards away, her head bloody, a tiny child huddled beside her, wailing. The guns were still roaring and all was confusion, flame and smoke belching from the doorways and windows of hastily vacated dwellings. Riders were racing their mounts through the aldea, shooting at anything that moved, animals as well as humans.

'Bandidos,' breathed the taller Texan. 'Now why d'you suppose they'd raid a little no-account place like Inagua?'

'We'll maybe find out later,' muttered Larry. 'C'mon. The stable's thisaway — I think.'

More dust-clouds assailed them. And then, directly ahead and advancing on them fast, they saw two of the raiders leading a couple of riderless horses, familiar animals. Before putting their torches to the barn, the raiders had commandered every likely horse, plus the saddles. Larry's sorrel was wearing Stretch's saddle, only one of its cinches buckled. Stretch's pinto wore Larry's saddle. In fury, and in fluent and explosive Spanish, Larry bellowed to the bandidos to release the sorrel and pinto. The two riders promptly leveled their pistols and the case-hardened drifters showed them no mercy. Their Colts roared. The horse-thieves were dead before they toppled from their mounts.

'You hear any more shootin'?' frowned Stretch.

'Nary a shot,' said Larry, cocking an ear to the hoofbeats. 'They've had their fun and now they're movin' out.'

Leading their horses, they trudged to the town square. The raiding party, forty or more riders, raised dust to the east. The smoke still weaved but the dust was clearing, the havoc visible to all sides, Inagua was a shambles of burning frame buildings and battered

5

adobes. They counted seven bodies sprawled in the dust, three of them female.

'Loco bastards!' scowled Stretch.

'Uh huh. Kill-crazy,' nodded Larry. 'They weren't here to loot. This was a murder raid.'

Until 3.30 that afternoon, the tall Americanos helped as best they could the mourning and wounded of tiny Inagua. They helped put out fires, worked rough surgery on men, women, even children, victims of the murder-lust of the bandit-pack. When they had done as much as they could do, they prepared to ride on.

Fat Bernadino came to them when they were switching their saddles. Wearily, he thanked them.

'For what?' grouched Larry. 'Hell, amigo, if we'd been wide awake when them bandidos rode in, we'd have cut loose with our rifles, might've downed maybe a half-dozen of 'em.'

'Might've saved a few lives,' sighed the taller Texan.

'Didn't get around to payin' for our lunch and the room,' said Larry, digging out his wallet.

Bernadino half-heartedly protested when Larry thrust a $50.00 bill at him.

'Too much, senor!'

'We got plenty,' Larry said gruffly. 'And you got a need.'

Plenty was putting it mild. Thanks to recent assistance from Dame Fortune, these compulsive nomads had scored heavily at the games of chance in the saloons and casinos of the Arizona Territory; at this time they were solvent to the tune of some $1,200.00, give or take a dollar or two.

Wistfully, the fat man watched them secure their Winchesters, saddlebags and packrolls and get mounted. They were eager to be gone, feeling they were intruding on Inagua's grief, but Larry was born curious. He fished out his makings and, as he rolled a cigarette, asked, 'You got any idea why? Why would that many bandidos hit a town

7

like this? They didn't steal nothin' but horses and only a few at that. The way it looked to us, they only craved to hurt and kill. Why?'

'We have suffered punishment,' mumbled Bernadioo. 'Ah, si. This is how El Capitan, punishes those who defy him.'

'He's called El Capitan, huh?' prodded Stretch. 'The sonofabitch that bosses these killers?'

'Only some of them raided Inagua,' shrugged Bernadino. 'I have heard it said and I believe it. There are many more. A hundred, senor. Maybe more. Quien sabe?'

'Punishment for what?' demanded Larry.

'Two days ago, some of these bandidos came to our aldea and tell us El Capitan will bring his raiding parties here for the water and for such supplies as they wish. We tell them no. We say there will be no welcome for thieves and asesinos in Inagua.' The fat man's shoulders slumped in defeat.

'We were foolish, si? Better for us if we pretend to admire these carrion?'

'It's your town,' frowned Larry. 'You folks got a right to keep the trail-trash out.'

'But we are not strong enough,' lamented Bernadino.

'Uh huh,' grunted Larry. 'And there's no bandido so lowdown as the kind who attack folks too weak to defend 'emselves.'

'Cut any of these bandidos — and they'll bleed yellow,' opined Stretch.

In the prevailing heat of late afternoon, their mood grim, the strife-weary Texans began putting distance between themselves and the shambles that had been a peaceful Mexican village. Drifting into Sonora to rest a while had seemed a good idea. Now, they pushed northeast for the New Mexico Territory, craving to put American land under the plodding hooves of their animals.

'Too bad there's just me and you,' complained the taller Texan. 'If we were a whole posse from the old Lone Star with plenty hardware, it'd be a real pleasure to wipe out this El Capitan buzzard, him and all his woman-killin' scum.'

Woodville Emerson, nicknamed Stretch for his stringy but powerful six and a half feet frame, was usually the easy-going, guileless half of this much-traveled duo. Like Larry, he favored the rig of the working Texas cowhand, but there all resemblance ended. His mane was as blond as Larry's was dark. And Handsome? He was not exactly that, not with his lantern jaw, too-wide mouth and jug-handle ears. Since Appomattox, he had been the tag-along, riding in Larry's shadow, content to leave all the heavy figuring, the brain-work, to his more mentally-agile sidekick.

Lawrence Valentine, often called 'runt' by Stretch because of his lesser height — he was a mere 6 feet 3 inches — was brawny about the shoulders and chest, but trim-waisted, a husky, sometimes cynical, sometimes sour-tempered nomad who, like Stretch, had seen a great deal of mayhem in the years since the war's end. Handsome in a rugged, battered, heavy-jawed way, he had come to resent their hex. Hexed they undoubtedly were, because, way back when they surrendered to their wanderlust, they had craved only to see the frontier and to socialize and sometimes befriend its new inhabitants, the cattle and farm folk, the townfolk, the mining communities. Outlaw-fighting and trouble-shooting had been far from their minds. Peace and quiet was all they sought; this they insisted to the point of monotony to any who would listen.

So much for good intentions. Within a month of quitting Texas, they had become embroiled in a shootout with bank bandits. A few months later, they had stumbled upon a stage hold-up and, though outnumbered, had forced the road agents to cut and run. From those early days until now, they had been shot at, knifed, gunwhipped, menaced by every breed of frontier malefactor, the bunko-steerers as well as the homicidal gun-slingers, the master criminals as well as their hire-lings. And still they survived, their hard-muscled bodies criss-crossed with the scars of a hundred or more battles from which they had emerged to fight again, which was more than could be said for their adversaries. For many, a clash with the Texas Trouble-Shooters was a one-way ticket to Boot Hill. For as many others, it meant trial, conviction and a long hitch in a state or territorial penitentiary.

'We're a couple Jonahs, and that's the ever-lovin' truth,' Stretch sourly asserted. 'Inagua was a peaceful town till we decided to rest our butts there. It was our lousy hex brought them bandidos down on them peaceable citizens.'

'Not this time,' countered Larry. 'This time, it was a big shot calls himself El Capitan, a sonofabitch renegade with a mean streak.'

Nothing more was said until they were camped by a waterhole 15 miles from the southwesternmost corner of New Mexico. Stretch, munching on sowbelly and beans without relish, stared wistfully into their fire and remarked, 'I guess we ain't that good, huh? Just the two of us — to go up against El Capitan's whole gang? We couldn't be that good?'

'We're good,' said Larry, grinning wryly. 'And we've had a lot of Lone Star luck in our time. But we're only human, ol'buddy. We can't work miracles.'

'That'd really be somethin' though, wouldn't it?' mused Stretch. 'The whole dirty, lowdown, trigger-happy, backshootin' outfit wiped out — the whole hundred. I mean, what's the best thing could happen to owlhoot trash that turns their guns on unarmed men, on women, on kids?'

'To get wiped out,' said Larry.

'That's what I mean,' nodded Stretch.

'So — uh — couldn't we think about it? We could do that much, couldn't we? Just think about it?'

'Think about it?' Larry grimaced irritably. 'I don't know how we're ever gonna forget it anyway.'

★ ★ ★

Toward noon of the next day, along the stage trail to the seat of Rodriguez County in the territory of New Mexico, three amateur desperadoes, petty thieves of no account, made a futile atempt to rob the Rodriguez-bound coach.

After rounding a bend of the regular route, the stage-driver cursed in exasperation and began stalling his team. So suddenly did the vehicle jerk to a halt that the passengers were jolted from their seats. The guard was at once alert, thumbing back the hammers on his double-barreled shotgun. The southwest-bound had come to a narrow section of the trail, and now that section was blocked by a stalled wagon. The crew couldn't see the team, only the rear of the vehicle and the unprepossessing character standing beside the trail, waving to them.

He was Mexican, fairly young and grinning blandly, flashing white teeth. But still unprepossessing, his black brows curving around his gleaming eyes. There were dark shadows under those eyes, so the general effect was unfortunate, pretty much as though he were studying them directly after a brawl in which he had suffered two black eyes.

'Saludos, Americanos!' he leered.

'Saludos yourself, and what the hell's the idea of blockin' the trail?' challenged the driver.

'He ain't armed,' observed the guard. 'What d'you make of this?'

His question was answered a second later and, for a few moments thereafter, driver and guard doubted the evidence of their eyes. A Mexican inside the wagon had thrown up the rear flaps to reveal a weapon guaranteed to demoralize any sane man who found himself facing it at short range — or even long range. The driver recognized it.

'Great day in the mornin'! They got a Gatling gun!'

The Mex crouched behind the Gatling chuckled triumphantly.

'Si!' he cried. 'Gataling — por cierto! I make him fire many times!'

Up front of the Conestoga, the unseen Mex on the driver's seat sniggered shrilly, chanting, 'We got a Gataling, we got a Gataling . . . !'

'Silencio!' ordered the man by the trail, and the sniggering ceased. 'And now, senors, you will obey my orders.' He gestured melodramatically. 'When I will count to three, you will please drop the shotgun and the cashbox . . . '

'Ain't haulin' no cashbox this run,' growled the driver. 'And that's a fact. If you think I'm lyin', you can climb up here and take a look.'

'No cashbox?' frowned the boss-thief.

'No cashbox,' said the driver.

'That is a disappointment,' complained the boss-thief. 'I am muy melancolico.'

'Tough,' jeered the guard.

'Careful, Ernie,' begged the driver. 'Don't smart-talk him. Not while his buddy's got that devil-gun ponted right at us.'

The boss-thief whipped off his sombrero and reversed it.

'The passengers will get out of the coach,' he commanded. 'I will collect their dinero and all other treasures. If they are still inside the coach after I have count to three, I will order my compadre to fire the Gataling . . . '

'You mean Gatling,' the guard dared correct him.

'That's what I said!' retorted the boss-thief. 'Gataling! And now I commence to count!'

The learing, squint-eyed rogue manning the Gatling chose this moment to call a remark to his companeros. Unfortunately for him, also for his

17

companeros, he resorted to his native tongue.

'Hey, Mapache, my friend! We are too clever for these gringos, are we not?'

The boss-thief chided him, also reverting to Spanish.

'Be quiet, Bobo. Just stay with the devil-gun and try to show these fools a murderous expression.'

'Aha, if only they knew!' chuckled Bobo. 'If only they knew we cannot fire the devil-gun — because something inside of it is broken!'

'Come out, todo el mundo!' ordered Mapache. 'Or I will order my amigo to shoot on you, and the Gataling will blow big holes through the coach and you will all die — muy pronto!' He began counting. 'One . . . !'

His jaw sagged. He winced in agitation because, so far, only one passenger was climbing out. That passenger was male, a lean, cold-eyed man in town clothes topped off by a broad-brimmed hat. He wasn't raising his hands. In fact, he hefted a cocked six-shooter in his right hand and the glint of the weapon's barrel was as intimidating as the gleaming of the badge of his vest. Three misfit opportunists had run out of luck, thanks to Bobo's big mouth. The lean man now threatening them was Deputy Sheriff Burl Dodson of Rodriguez County, who happened to be fluent in Spanish.

'You up front — and you inside!' He bellowed to the other hold-up artists while drawing a bead on Mapache's belly. 'Get your butts outa that wagon in a hurry!'

To emphasize his command, he repeated it in Spanish. Bobo and the third thief, a swarthy loser only 5 feet 1 inch tall, obeyed in nervous haste. The stage-driver gasped a question.

'How'd you bluff 'em, Dodson? And them with a Gatling?'

'I savvy Spanish,' growled the depty. 'Heard the bobo say it's busted — so they couldn't fire it anyway.'

The guard called an assurance to the other passengers; in just a few minutes, they would be on their way again. And a few minutes was all it took. The deputy made short work of securing the inept road agents, using his manacles and a coil of rope provided by the crew. He heaved them into the wagon one by one, then climbed to the seat and whipped up the 4-horse team.

An hour later, the wagon was accommodated in the high-fenced yard behind the Rodriguez County Jail and Sheriff's Office. The yard also boasted a pole corral in which the team now rested. Deputy Dodson was making the return journey from Alamogordo after delivering a prisoner when Mapache and his cronies held up the stage, which proved their timing was no better than their luck.

Sheriff Cy Marlowe's other deputy, beefy Gus Hines, perched on a stool by the cellblock entrance and grinned derisively at the disgruntled trio now being interrogated by his chief. Leaner than Dodson, his disposition soured by the demands of his job, the balding Marlowe surveyed them grimly and demanded answers to his questions. Dodson stood by after searching their shabby peons' outfits and coming up with nothing, not one thin dime. Marlowe led off by demanding the prisoners identify themselves.

'I am called Mapache . . . ' began that one.

'And you're well-named,' jibed Dodson. 'You sure as hell *look* like a racoon.'

'Mapache who?' frowned Marlowe.

'Quien sabe?' Mapache shrugged apologetically. 'We know nothing of our padres and less of our madres — you understand?'

'Three dumb bastards!' guffawed Hines.

'And your amigos?' prodded Marlowe.

'The little one is called Pepi and the foolish one is Bobo,' offered Mapache.

'Three dumb bastards, every one a fool,' grinned Hines.

'All right, you fearless bandidos . . . ' began Marlowe.

'Hey, Cy, could they be three of El Capitan's riders?' wondered Hines.

'Gus, that's a stupid question,' muttered Dodson. 'You never saw the day Carrizo would recruit three such no-accounts. Every Carrizo rider is a top gun and plenty smart.'

'Next question . . . ' The sheriff stared hard at the prisoners. 'Where'd you get the Gatling?'

'We borrow the Gataling . . . ' began Mapache.

'Stole,' corrected Marlowe.

'From where the gringo soldados are camped,' said Mapache.

'Mesa Valdez?' Marlowe asked incredulously.

'Si, Senor Sheriff.'

'How in blazes did three loco thieves — fools like you — manage to steal a Gatling from an army post?'

As offered by Mapache, the explanation was absurdly simple, also a mite confusing. It was an important fiesta

22

for the gringos, July 4th, when these raggletail scavengers scouted the army post in hopes of purloining provisions, liquor, anything of value. They admired the Gatling after breaking into the armory. How did they manage this without drawing attention to themselves? No trouble at all. The officers and men of Mesa Valdez were celebrating the Glorious 4th — enthusiastically. A fire broke out in a mess-shack a goodly distance from the armory. It seemed everything was going their way when almost the entire company began fighting the fire. They loaded the Gatling and ammunition into the wagon and . . .

'What wagon?' scowled Marlowe. 'That's no army vehicle. I know a Conestoga when I see one. Where'd you get the wagon?'

'Santa Clara — no?' frowned Bobo.

'No,' grunted Pepi. 'Arroya Rojo.'

'Toledo Bend,' Mapache corrected them, exasperated. He nodded to the lawmen and touched his temple. 'Be patient with my compadres. They are not as smart as Mapache.'

'In Toledo Bend, who'd you steal the rig and team from?' asked Marlowe.

'Quien sabe?' shrugged Mapache. 'The carreta was empty and the caballos in harness. We drive out of Toledo Bend. Nobody is objectionable. Nobody shoots at us.'

'They came a long way, these damn prairie dogs,' Marlowe remarked to his deputies. 'Returning their loot is gonna be quite a chore.'

'Damn right,' agreed Dodson. 'Mesa Valdez is a fair trace from here and Toledo Bend's farther still — and we don't know who owns the wagon.'

'Well now . . . ' Marlowe eyed the shabby trio coldly. 'You're gonna have plenty time for wishing you hadn't stole the wagon or the Gatling or anything else. Circuit-judge held court here two days ago, which means he won't be here again for six weeks or more. That's six weeks for you to bunk in the one cell and . . . '

'We get to eat gringo food, si?' Bobo asked eagerly. 'I like gringo food!'

'I like *any* food,' mumbled Pepi. 'My belly is muy vacio.'

'Oh, you'll eat,' sneered Hines. 'Got to keep up your strength, so you won't faint in court when we read the charges against you.'

'Theft of a wagon and army weaponry — plus ammunition,' growled Marlowe. 'And armed hold-up. You threatened the stage-crew and the passengers with that damn Gatling.'

'When'd you trash find out it wouldn't work?' demanded Hines.

'We try to shoot it one day after we borrow it,' sighed Mapache.

'But you had the gall to try a hold-up anyway,' muttered Dodson. 'And the bobo tipped your hand, babblin' in your own lingo.'

'Take 'em in, Gus,' ordered Marlowe. 'They'll be lousy company for Homer.' With a wry grin, he added, 'Tell Homer I'll apologize to him later.'

After Hines had hustled the prisoners

into the jailhouse, Dodson seated himself and asked, 'Homer who?'

'Gledhill, the gunsmith,' said Marlowe.

The deputy's eyesbrows shot up.

'How'd Homer Gledhill ever get himself arrested? What's the charge? Hell, Cy, he'd have to be one of the hardest-workin', most inoffensive citizens in all of Rodriquez County!'

'Every man has his breaking point,' Marlowe said sagely. 'Homer's married to his.'

'Meanin' that wife of his?' frowned Dodson.

'Every time I catch sight of Theodora Gledhill, I give thanks for my wife's easy disposition,' said the sheriff. 'She is one vinegar-tempered female, that Theodora. And, since her mother came to live with them, you can bet it's been worse for Homer. Instead of just the wife making his life miserable, there's fat old Hester Plumrose to throw in her ten cents worth.'

'I reckon I'll stay bachelor,' sighed Dodson. 'What'd Homer do anyway?'

'It'll be an assault charge,' said Marlowe.

'Homer paddled his wife's fat backside?' grinned Dodson. 'Well, more power to him. It couldn't happen to a more deservin' case.'

'What happened was he blacked Theodora's eye,' said Marlowe. 'Then Theodora's mother started hollering at him. There was this pie on the kitchen table and . . .'

'What kind?'

'I'd guess apple — from the way old Hester looked when I arrived. Yeah, you just know what he did. Picked up that platter and rammed the whole damn pie in the old lady's kisser.'

Dodson had one regret and he expressed it with heavy sincerity.

'I wish I'd seen that.'

'But it's a hollow victory for Homer,' declared Marlowe, whose vocabulary was better than average for that time. 'He's lost his spirit, Burl. Doesn't much care what happens to him now.

I'd say his marriage is as dead as Davy Crockett.'

'Then he oughtn't be pinin',' asserted Dodson. 'If I was him, I'd be feelin' like celebratin'.'

Two days later, 3 o'clock of another hot and dry afternoon, the Texans drifted into Rodriquez and, after a lazy progress along the main street, dismounted in front of the Broken Spur Saloon and looped their reins to the hitch-rail. Into the saloon they trudged, saddlesore and thirsty. And, for once, their sixth sense was failing them, their instinct for danger letting them down. While idling their mounts along the street, they had won the attention of an excited Deputy Hines.

A few moments later, emerging from a barber shop. Burl Dodson was accosted by his colleague.

'We got a couple live ones, Burl, and this is a chore for the both of us. I just now spotted 'em. Real rough hombres — and wanted bad.'

'Who — where . . . ?'

'In the Broken Spur. Looked like they'd ridden quite a ways, so they ain't about to quit in a hurry. Gives us time to fetch shotguns. They fit the dscription, Burl. We got a bulletin while you were gone to Alamogordo.'

On their way to the office, Hines offered further details. The two strangers tallied with the description on the handbill circulating from Lawson City, a sizeable town far to the north. One Maxwell Tatlock, chief cashier of Lawson City's Southern & Pacific Bank, had taken a good long look at the tall men who had brazenly withdrawn $5000.00 at gunpoint, shooting and wounding the manager in the process. And neglecting to cover their faces.

'They were the tallest men ever seen in that town,' said Hines. 'And these two are the tallest I ever saw in *this* town. I've pegged 'em good, Burl. They gotta be the same two.'

'You're probably right,' agreed Dodson. 'And, if they're all that trigger-happy, we're gonna have to handle this carefully.'

'We'll get the drop on 'em,' decided Hines.

'The only way,' nodded Dodson.

The cheerful barkeep with the close-cropped hair and Teutonic features, Fritz Sondheim by name, was quite a mine of information and only too willing to satisfy the Texans' curiosity about the infamous El Capitan. Also, he was inquisitive.

'How come you're interested?' he demanded, as he refilled their tankards.

'We were visitin' across the border,' offered Larry. He took a pull at his beer and fished out his makings. 'Little town in Sonora.'

'Place called Inagua,' said Stretch. 'And, while we were there, a bunch of bandidos came a'raidin'.'

'Some of El Capitan's gunhawks,' muttered Larry.

'Gents, be thankful you got out of that town alive,' said Sodheim.

'We're thankful, Fritz,' Larry assured him. 'But them Mexicans back in

Inagua, they got nothin' to be thankful for.'

Sondheim launched into a terse but comprehensive account of the known depredations of Northern Mexico's newest threat and confided all he had heard of the wild ambitions of the boss-bandido. Real name Ricardo Carrizo. An arrogant plunderer with big ideas.

'Claims he needs all the cash he can get his greasy paws on — dollars, pesos or gold — to finance his great dream.'

'His great dream,' Larry repeated in disgust.

'Wait till you hear this,' muttered the barkeep. 'He wants all that cash so he can bribe the Federales to throw in with him when he reaches Mexico City. I'm tellin' you Carrizo plans on runnin' President Juan Melgosa right out of the palace and takin' over. That's a fact. Carrizo craves to make himself the next president of Mexico.'

'I'll be damned,' breathed Stretch.

'They hit fast and hard, El Capitan's raiders,' declared Sondheim. 'Both sides of the border. Towns in Arizona, couple towns right here in the New Mexico Territory. No guessin' where they'll strike next. And there's better than a hundred of 'em. So you can see how it is. That big a gang is gonna be hard to beat.' He shrugged philosophically. 'Still, I guess they'll tangle with the Second Cavalry sooner or later, and that'll be the end of 'em.'

When their informant moved away to assist the other barkeep, Larry lit his cigarette and scowled morosely. Stretch downed a mouthful of cold beer, smacked his lips and wistfully opined, 'It'd be worth riskin' our hides for.'

'What?' frowned Larry.

'You know what I mean,' said Stretch. 'Catchin' up with that killer gang, givin' El Capitan his come-uppance. It'd be a rough chore, but sure worth the trouble.'

'We'll take care of it soon as we finish these beers,' Larry sarcastically suggested. 'After all, there's only a hundred of 'em, so what're we waitin' for?'

'No use talkin' down to me,' chided Stretch. 'It's what you crave, and you know it.'

'It's what I crave,' Larry admitted. 'But I haven't got around to figurin' how just two Texans can lick a hundred bandidos.'

He tensed then, and so did Stretch. The muzzles of shotguns were suddenly rammed against their backbones.

# 2

## Guests of Rodriguez County

The trouble-shooters placed their hands on the bar and raised their eyes to the mirror above the shelves, the better to inspect their challengers. Thoughtfully, they studied the tense faces of the deputies, while other customers warily sidestepped and the barkeeps, table-hands and percentage women froze where they stood. Dodson's shotgun was menacing the taller Texan. Hines' was prodding Larry.

'We'd as soon get this done quietly,' muttered Dodson. 'Crowded saloon, boys. Bad place for tryin' a break. Bad place for gunplay.'

'I'll allow you're talkin' sense,' drawled Larry. 'But them cannons don't make no sense at all.'

'Real cool, ain't they?' jeered Hines.

'You're under arrest — suspicion of bank robbery,' said Dodson. 'We'll be holdin' you in the county jail while a cashier comes to check the identification. If this other officer is wrong about you, you got nothin' to worry about. Now slip your holster-ties and unstrap your guns — slow and careful.'

'What d'you make of this, runt?' frowned Stretch.

'This close to a couple shotguns, we're in a bad position for arguin',' opined Larry. 'The lard-belly looks jumpy. A nervous badge-toter with a cocked scattergun is my idea of a bad combination.'

He disarmed himself and, shrugging resignedly, Stretch followed his example. Sondheim was ordered to come round from behind the bar, pick up the gunbelts and hang them over Dodson's shoulder. This he did, eyeing the tall men with renewed interest and enquiring, 'Did you fellers really rob a bank?'

'No,' said Larry. 'But I got a hunch these shotgunners'll be hard to convince.'

'We move out now,' Dodson said briskly.

Outside the saloon, Larry nodded to their horses.

'What about our animals? We didn't take time to stable 'em.'

'They'll be kept in the jailyard,' said Dodson. 'We got a corral.'

He called to a passing townman to untie the sorrel and pinto and follow to the sheriff's office. The Texans moved off with the deputies at their heels, the cocked shotguns still prodding them, the townman following with the horses.

'You ain't sore yet,' Stretch quietly accused. 'How about it? You *ever* gonna get sore about this?'

'With a shotgun at my back, I never get sore,' muttered Larry. 'We know we don't rob banks. So we should fret?'

After delivering the horses to the jailyard, the same local was asked to summon the sheriff.

'But first, offsaddle those animals and bring the gear to the office,' urged Dodson.

When Marlowe came hustling in, the strangers had emptied their pockets and been searched by Dodson, with Hines' shotgun still at the ready.

'That bulletin from Lawson City,' Hines told his boss. 'Check it and you'll see why I nailed these hombres.'

'With a little help from another deputy,' growled Dodson.

After a frowning appraisal of the impassive Texans, the sheriff went to a file cabinet for the bulletin. He scanned it, then studied them intently.

'You gonna tell us you were never in Lawson City?' he challenged. 'The way it looks to me, Deputy Hines is dead right about you.'

'We don't even know Lawson City,' said Larry. 'We rode northeast from Sonora these past few days.'

'Cash, Cy,' said Dodson, inspecting the contents of Larry's wallet. 'They're

rigged like ranch-hands, but totin'
mucho dinero.'

'Count it,' ordered Marlowe.

He returned the bulletin to the
cabinet and moved around the desk to
sag into his chair. Patiently he waited,
his eyes on the tall men.

'Eleven hundred, thirty-two dollars
— exactly,' reported Dodson.

'Hang their hardware on the gunrack,
lock up the money, then check the
packrolls and saddlebags,' said Marlowe.

'While your deputies are snoopin' in
our gear, you want to tell us about this
bank we didn't rob?' asked Larry.

'Real cool thieves,' chuckled Hines.

'Lawson City,' Marlowe told the
Texans. 'The Southern and Pacific
bank. We'll send for the cashier, feller
name of Tatlock, to come identify you.
Happens he got a clear look at you,
and . . .'

'At the men who robbed him,'
countered Larry.

'And shot his boss,' retorted Marlowe.
'Better set your minds to it. We'll

be holding you four days or more. No stage service from Lawson to Rodriguez, so Tatlock has to make it on horseback or in a rig of some kind. I'd say it'd take him all of four days.'

'Look at it this way,' offered Dodson. 'If Tatlock never saw you before, we apologize and turn you loose. You've lost nothin' but time.'

'Well, that's plumb fortunate for us,' shrugged Stretch, 'on account of time is what we got plenty of.'

'Names?' frowned Marlowe.

'Never saw us before, huh?' prodded Larry.

'All I know about you and your partner is you're taller than most,' said Marlowe. 'That makes you conspicuous.'

'Makes us *what?*' asked Stretch, blinking worriedly.

'And that's the tie-up,' Marlowe went on. 'Tatlock claims he never saw men so tall. So can you blame me for holding you on suspicion? Now, about those names . . . ?'

'He's Woodville, I'm Lawrence,' said Larry.

'And, just so we'll all understand one another,' muttered Stretch. 'We don't take kindly to the idea of stewin' in a calaboose for what some other hombres did. Just happens we ain't partial to bank robbers — or any other kind of owlhoot.'

'Well, shucks . . . !' Hines chuckled scathingly. 'As well as arrestin' these no-accounts, we're hurtin' their feelin's!'

'That's enough, Gus,' chided Marlowe. 'You and Burl take them in now — so I can get back to the meeting.'

'Where's the meetin' and what's it all about?' asked Dodson, unhitching his keyring.

'Mayor Finn's office,' growled Marlowe. 'And the object of the meeting is to discuss just how well defended this town is — against the danger of a raid.'

'El Capitan's bunch?' frowned Hines. 'You think they'd try a raid on *our* town?'

'Carrizo is unpredictable — to put it mildly,' shrugged Marlowe. 'No guessing what he'll do. Go on, boys. Let them keep their tobacco and matches.' He warned the Texans, 'Last prisoner who tried to create a diversion by setting fire to his blankets, all we did was throw water at him. A lot of water.'

'Damn fool near drowned,' recalled Hines. 'Took him two days to get dry again.'

Keeping their indignation in check, the Texans submitted to the indignity of being locked into the double cell. It had all happened before and maybe they should have been accustomed to it by now. In too many cowtowns and mining camps they had been obliged to defend themselves against local hard cases, the kind whose favorite pastime was prodding strangers into a fight in a saloon. Usually on such occasions, the town marshal or county sheriff tended to favor the locals and arrest the out of-towners for disturbing the peace, not to mention breaking a nose or two; the Lone Star Hellions were hard to beat in a barroom brawl.

They retreated to the bunks, flopped and traded stares with the occupants of the opposite cells, the three unkempt Mexicans sharing accommodation, a doleful-looking, heavyset man alone in the adjoining cell. The jailhouse door clanged shut. They rolled and lit cigarettes, ignored the Mexicans and traded nods with the heavyset man. He was clean-shaven, his work-clothes in fair condition, his thick thatch showing flecks of grey.

'Howdy,' said Stretch. 'What do we call you?'

'Homer.' The name was offered in tones that suggested its owner was ashamed of it. 'Homer Gledhill.'

'Saludos, amigos!' beamed Mapache.

He identified himself and compadres, but the Texans showed little interest.

'We're Lawrence and Woodville,' Larry told Homer.

'If that's what you want to call

yourselves, it's fine by me.' Homer shrugged unconcernedly. 'I won't let on.'

'Howzat again?' frowned Stretch. 'Aw, hell! They got a newspaper in this town!'

'No newspaper in Rodriguez, but we get the Alamogordo paper once in a while,' said Homer. 'Sure, I've read of you and seen your pictures. But, like I said, that's your business. And, if *I* had such a reputation, I sure wouldn't use *my* real name.'

'I just told you our real names,' said Larry.

'Sure,' nodded Homer. 'What're you in for?'

'Couple tall hombres robbed a bank in a town called Lawson,' said Larry. He went on to repeat his futile attempts to convince the local law of their mistake, then remarked, 'It could be worse for us. At least the cashier's comin' down from Lawson to identify us.'

'Which he can't,' Stretch pointed

out, 'on account of he never saw us before. Just two other tall hombres.'

'Then they'll have to turn us loose,' said Larry.

'We are desperadoes!' bragged Bobo, eager to impress the tall Texans. 'We hold up the stagecoach!'

'Like hell,' scoffed Stretch.

'Is true, amigos!' insisted Pepi.

'You ain't gonna believe how these lamebrains got to be guests of the county,' Homer said with a wry grin.

'You got an honest face, Homer,' said Larry. 'Any way you tell it, we'll have to believe it.'

'They stole a wagon at Toledo Bend, took it to the army post at Mesa Valdez and stole a Gatling gun — plus plenty ammunition,' muttered Homer. After trading frowns, the Texans fixed dubious eyes on the leering Mexicans. 'Yeah, it's hard to believe. I wouldn't have believed it, but, last time Burl Dodson took me out back to use the privy, he let me check it over. It's a Gatling, sure enough. Lucky for

Mapache it can't be fired, else him and his buddies'd be up on a murder charge. That Gatling uses sixty-five calibre cartridges. Can you imagine how it might've been if they'd got it workin'? One burst could plumb perforate a stagecoach and everybody in it.'

Still studying the Mexicans, Larry protested, 'They look too damn loco to get away with it.'

'Stealin' a Gatling from an army post?' blinked Stretch. '*Them?*'

'Any other time, they'd have been inside the guardhouse pretty damn quick,' opined Homer. 'But it was Fourth of July, the whole regiment celebratin' — you know?'

'Somethin' I'm curious about, Homer,' said Larry. 'It ain't every citizen can check a Gatling and see what's wrong with it. How come you savvy Gatlings?'

'I'm a gunsmith,' said Homer. 'Never worked on a Gatling, but I could if I had to. They sure like to

45

brag, those gun-makers. Send manuals to gunsmiths all over the country. Advertisin', they call it.' He squatted by his cell-door and stared gloomily in the general direction of the jailyard. 'I could do the army a favor. With that manual and my tools, why, I bet I could fix their Gatling in just a few hours. Not that I'm special partial to soldiers.'

'We should own such a gun,' Larry remarked.

'Oh, sure,' nodded Stretch. 'Then we'd have us an edge, maybe wipe out El Capitan's whole army.'

'Heard of those killers, have you?' prodded Homer.

'Tangled with 'em before we knew who they were,' said Larry. He briefly described the Inagua raid and, moodily eyeing Mapache and his cohorts, declared, 'Trigger-happy Mex renegades're the worst kind of trash.'

'We are not trash,' Mapache was quick to protest. 'We are caballeros. Bandidos, si, but caballeros too.'

46

'El Capitan — muy malo — muy depravado,' mumbled Pepi, wincing. 'I am freeze in my belly when I hear his name.'

'I would kill him for the price on his head,' bragged Mapache. 'But how would I find him by himself? He has a hundred men. Maybe more!'

'Twenty thousand United States dollars,' said Homer. 'A year ago, the territorial governments of Arizona and New Mexico were offerin' five thousand. That'll give you an idea how much strife he's caused in just one year.'

'Homer, you know how we got arrested, us and the bobos,' said Stretch. 'You gonna tell us what *you're* doin' in this calaboose?'

Homer sighed and bowed his head.

'I was hopin' you'd forget to ask, you Texans with all your chivalry and such. Yeah. I ain't forgettin' your reputation.'

'Now, Homer, what could a friendly hombre like you do that we'd disapprove of?' challenged Larry. 'I bet you're just as chivalrous as us.'

'Always was,' Homer gloomily assured him. 'Took all the rantin' and naggin' they gave me, took it for a long time.'

'Rantin' and naggin' from who?' asked Stretch.

'First Theodora, my wife, then Mrs Hester Plumrose, her mother,' said Homer. 'And then both of 'em.'

'The old lady moved in with you, huh?' prodded Stretch.

'About a week ago — well — I got good and mad, kind of lost my head,' Homer confessed. 'If a man calls himself a man, damn it, he can only abide so much. I just couldn't take it any more, all the criticizin' and the complainin', day in and day out.'

'Homer, if you want to get it off your chest, go ahead,' offered Larry. 'But, if you'd as soon not talk of it, that's fine by us. We don't want to pry.'

Even so, Homer blurted it out.

'I hit Theodora in the eye, gave her an awful shiner . . . !'

'For shame, Homer!' protested Stretch, shocked to the core.

'But that's only the half of it!' gasped Homer. 'I picked up the apple pie — a whole apple pie — and shoved it right in my mother-in-law's ugly face! So how d'you like *that?*'

'Hell, runt, that's terrible!' breathed Stretch.

'Maybe — and maybe not.' Larry was Southern chivalrous to the backbone, but a realist too, willing to make allowances for exceptional provocation. 'Every man has his reasons, and I figure Homer had his.'

'I already told you my reason,' muttered Homer. 'They never let up, not Theodora or that old sow Hester. Always belittlin' me, always talkin' me down, always claimin' Theodora married a poor provider. That's what they call me — a poor provider . . . !'

'Uh — now — don't get riled up, Homer . . . ' begged Stretch.

'Been a gunsmith most of my life!' raged Homer. 'You want to know how old I was when my old Uncle Julius started teachin' me the trade? Twelve is all I was. And I learned good. But were those women ever gonna be satisfied? Never! I don't savvy business, they claim. Not enough money comin' in . . . '

'Cool down, ol' buddy,' soothed Larry. 'We ain't ashamed to call you 'friend.' Right, stringbean?'

'Right.' Stretch nodded vehemently. 'Any man who'll clobber a naggin' woman and hit her ma with an apple pie — can't be all bad.'

'It took nerve and grit,' opined Larry.

'Every husband should be so brave,' asserted Stretch.

'What we call courage, Homer,' declared Larry.

'You think so?' Homer shrugged dejectedly. 'Well, I've been feelin' lowdown ever since it happened. Don't care what happens to me.'

'What will happen to you?' asked Larry.

'It's started already, I bet,' muttered Homer. 'I can just see 'em now — Theodora, the old sow, and Orville.'

'Who's Orville?' demanded Stretch.

'Orville Plumrose, my penny-pinchin' brother-in-law that owns the hardware store in the next block,' said Homer. 'Not enough profit to gunsmithin', he always says. Better I should've sold out to him so he could turn my place into another hardware store. So now they get what they always wanted. Two stores with the Plumrose name on the windows.'

'They'll just throw you out?' frowned Stretch. 'Can they do that?'

'What can I do to stop 'em?' sighed Homer. 'I'll be stuck in this jail six weeks before I have my day in court. Judge Hollander, he won't just fine me. Hell, no. With Theodora and the old sow whinin' of how I beat up on 'em, he'll sure as hell send me to the territorial prison.' Wistfully he confided, 'If there was any way I could bust out of this jail, get far away from

51

Rodriguez, I'd be the happiest man in the whole world. I'd just find me some quiet town, change my name and start all over again and I'd stay woman-shy the rest of my life — and like it.'

'You and Theodora had no kids,' guessed Larry.

'It's never been a real marriage,' scowled Homer. 'I think she started hatin' my guts the first night we were together, and that's how it's been ever since.'

Having unburdened himself, the gunsmith returned to his bunk to catnap fitfully. Mapache and his companeros hankered to engage the tall gringos in sociable conversation, but were intimidated by Larry's warning scowl. Sprawled on their bunks, the Texans pondered Homer's misery and mutually agreed that, in comparison, they had little cause for complaint. Soon enough they would be gone from this place. Soon enough, cashier Tatlock would come to Rodriguez, be ushered into this jail to look them over and would shake his head, no doubt disappointed that Marlowe and his deputies had been holding the wrong men.

Stretch was profoundly affected, overawed by the magnitude of Homer Gledhill's plight. His voice shook a little as he softly and fervently opined, 'There's just nothin' worse could happen to a man than be hogtied to a wife like Theodora.'

'Better a man cut his throat,' muttered Larry. 'Better still, *her* throat.'

'And the hell of it is,' mused Stretch, 'He's a right likeable feller. No meanness in him. Just a hard-toilin' gunsmith.'

'It always happens to the good men,' Larry supposed.

'We were right, huh?' suggested Stretch. 'I mean, way back when we first started driftin' and we told ourselves it'd be all wrong, a real bad deal, for the likes of us to try settlin' down — with a wife.'

'Wives,' corrected Larry. 'If ever we'd settled down, we'd have needed a wife apiece. But we were right, sure.'

An hour later, because they needed to relieve themselves, the new prisoners were escorted out back one at a time by Deputy Dodson, and this was Larry's first sight of the jailyard and its surroundings. Casually, never suspecting his memory of such details would work to his advantage, he noted the location of the corral housing the wagon team and his and Stretch's horses, their saddles resting on the toprail, the durable Conestoga with the muzzle of its fearsome cargo visible just inside the tailgate, and the two exits from the yard, a wider barred gate to the rear to permit passage of vehicles, a smaller gate in the fence to the right. He wasn't thinking of a breakout. The idea of a clean getaway from the Rodriguez County Jail did not occur to him until mid-morning three days later.

★ ★ ★

At 9.50 a.m. of the day no local would forget, Deputy Hines was minding the office, amusing himself by lounging in the open entrance to the cellblock and calling taunts. The Texans, he predicted, would be identified by the Lawson City bank-teller and, in due course, be tried and convicted. They could expect to grow old in a territorial penitentiary. Homer Gledhill, already despised and derided for his cruelty to his wife and mother-in-law, would be pelted with trash on his way to court, where the circuit-judge would undoubtedly impose a harsh sentence. As for those three loco greasers, it would be many a long year before they saw the outside of a penitentiary. No sneaking Mex bastards could steal army weapons and escape their just desserts.

Once, when Hines paused to take a breath, Homer gruffly remarked to the Texans, 'Gus Hines got a mean streak a yard wide — in case you haven't noticed.'

'Whoever pinned the badge on

that blubber-gutted sonofabitch, they must've been desperate for a segundo deputy,' Larry opined loud enough for Hines to hear.

At 10 a.m., the Rodriguez banks opened for business. Uptown at the Broken Spur and at the other saloons of the town, early customers drifted in for their first drink of the day. Main Street was as busy as was normal for this time, people patronizing the stores, old timers whittling in front of barber shops and livery stables, the small fry at their lessons in the county schoolhouse, willingly or otherwise, the professional gamblers completing their ablutions and giving some thought to their late breakfast, the bawds of the saloons and bordellos still sleeping.

On the porch of the town's best hotel, Sheriff Marlowe and Deputy Dodson socialized with townmen of their acquaintance. It promised to be another warm day. Five minutes later, the temperature became unbearable, all hell broke loose.

It began with startling suddenness, the riders charging into Main Street from north and south, sixty or more fast-moving Mexicans filling the air with gun-thunder. And those six-shooters weren't being discharged skyward in the manner of likkered-up payday cowhands; the bandidos fired on locals frantically dashing running for cover.

On the hotel porch, the lawmen ordered their friends to drop flat, then emptied their holsters and, with verandah-posts their only shield, opened fire on horsemen charging past. Other locals, more enraged that intimidated, took their cue from the lawmen and made haste to arm themselves. Some retreated into back alleys with the idea of climbing to roofs to fire down on the invaders. Others did their shooting from windows or the barricaded entrances to side alleys. At the schoolhouse, the children were ordered to huddle under their desks. In the churches of Rodriguez, clergy of several persuasions prayed for deliverance. All along Main Street the gun-thunder echoed, deafening, threatening. Bandidos charged their mounts through the front doorways of the banks and the looting began, bankers and their staff forced to unlock safes and vaults at gunpoint.

Following on the first outbreak of shooting. Gus Hines had slammed and locked and barred the street-door of the sheriff's office. His initial reaction would have won Cyrus Marlowe's approval, but his show of resistance was short-lived. From the window, he cut loose with his Colt at riders barely visible in the dust-clouds rising from pounding hooves. One of his bullets almost scored. A rider promptly wheeled his mount, yelled to his colleagues and began emptying a pistol toward the law office. A slug ricocheted off the window-ledge and upward to leave a jagged hole in the ceiling and, on its flight, missed the fat deputy's face by less than an inch.

That did it for Gus Hines. The color drained from his face as he backstepped across the office and into the jailhouse. In there, Larry was calling to Homer.

'Sorry about the women. This'll be El Capitan's band for sure. And we've seen how . . . '

'Theodora and her mother'll be safe enough,' Homer assured him. 'I know right where they are. In the cellar. And you can bet your Texas spurs brother Orville's in *his* cellar — that jelly-livered stuffshirt.'

'Why ain't you out front?' Stretch challenged the haggard and trembling Hines. 'From the window, you could get a clear shot . . . '

'You — dunno what it's like — out there?' gasped Hines. 'I never seen anything like this before! They're *everywhere!* Too many of 'em! Oh, hell . . . !'

'He's scared to his yellow backbone,' sneered Stretch.

'Senor Woodville, do not blame him

for his fears!' wailed Pepi. 'We are *all* afraid!'

'This town don't stand a chance against all them raiders,' mumbled Hines. He hurried to the rear door to ensure it was well and truly locked, then began pacing the passage, voicing his fears. 'I dunno how long this jail can last — against so many of 'em. We'll all be killed. Oh, hell! I don't wanta die!'

'What happened to your boss and the other deputy?' demanded Larry.

'I dunno where they are,' groaned Hines. 'Only thing I could do was lock and bar the street-door. I was shootin' from the window — sure I was — but I near got my head blowed off!'

The pacing continued along with the agitated mumbling. He had the full sympathy of the three Mexicans, but was earning the contempt of the veteran trouble-shooters, who regarded cowardice as a useless emotion at best — strictly non-productive. Equally disgusted was Homer, though he was stuck with his claim of not caring a damn about his own future.

From the side of his mouth, Larry muttered to Stretch.

'We ain't doin' anybody any good, stewin' in this cage. So, seein' as how Rodriguez is busy right now, this is our best chance of makin' a break.'

'Bust out of jail?' challenged Stretch. 'But, doggone it, that's as good as admittin' we're the hombres robbed that bank!'

'I'm countin' on the cashier clearin' us anyway,' said Larry. 'But why wait? On the loose, we could make ourselves useful — make a lot of trouble for these bandidos.'

'You mean . . . ?'

'I mean if we take the others with us. The Mexicanos to hitch up the team and drive the wagon. Homer to fix the Gatling. That's the only way we're gonna settle Carrizo's hash. We need that Gatling, need it workin'.'

'Well,' said Stretch. 'When you put it that way . . . '

The demoralized deputy shuffled by again and Larry's questing eyes traveled from his pasty, haggard face to his midriff and the keyring dangling from his pants-belt. He rose unhurriedly, moved to the cell-door and awaited his chance. Next time Hines came his way, he addressed him softly.

'Come listen to me, Deputy . . . '

The clamor of gunfire sounded closer now. Hines eyed him uncomprehendingly and complained, 'I can't hear a word you're sayin'.'

Larry raised his voice.

'I said you could come out of it alive. That's what you want, huh?' He crooked a finger. 'I'll explain it careful.'

Like a lamb to the slaughter, the flabby lawman stumbled into the trap, moving close enough for Larry's right hand to dart out and grasp his neckerchief. Larry hauled with all his might, simultaneously taking a quick step backward, and the consequences were painful for Hines, but only briefly.

62

His forehead slammed against the bars with stunning force. His eyes glazed and his legs buckled and Larry hung on, growling to his partner to come lend a hand. Stretch joined him, bent low and shoved an arm through the bars. To the consternation of Homer Gledhill, the befuddled deputy was allowed to flop in an untidy heap, but not before Stretch had unhitched his keyring.

'You mean to break jail?' he gasped. 'Damn it, Lawrence, you couldn't pick a worse time! We'll be shot at — soon as we show our noses outside of . . . !'

'I'll get this said fast,' called Larry. At his second attempt, he found the right key and turned it. 'We're all goin'. With these keys, I can get us to the yard out back — and out of it. We're takin' the wagon, Homer. And what's *in* it. You savvy?'

'You want the Gatling?' frowned Homer, as Larry hustle across to release him. 'But — what the hell for?'

'What the hell d'you think?' countered Larry. 'When Carrizo's killers quit

Rodriguez, there's a better than even chance they'll head for his headquarters. And that many riders will leave clear sign for us to follow.'

'Follow 'em all the way and . . . ?' Homer waxed sceptical, but did not hesitate to don his hat and quit his cell. 'Hell! That'd be suicide!'

'You're tired of livin' anyway,' Stretch reminded him while unlocking the Mexicans' cell. 'Don't care if you live or die you said.'

Hurrying to the rear door, Larry lifted the bar and tossed it aside. He checked the keys again and, moments later, was opening the door a few inches to scan the yard.

'All clear so far,' he observed. 'Homer, how far to your store?'

'It's this same side of Main.' Homer jerked a thumb. 'Down that way. Not far.' He shook his head incredulously. 'I swear you mean it. You want me to go get my toolbox.'

'And the manual,' grinned Larry. 'Give me a couple minutes.' He moved past the other escapees. 'Be right with you.'

En route to the office, he paused beside Hines, who was showing signs of reviving. This was no time for being slowed down by a fat deputy, he reasoned. And so he hauled Hines half-upright and swung a hard fist to the side of his head. Like a poleaxed steer, Hines went down again.

In the office, Larry repossessed his Colt, strapped it on and slung his partner's double-holstered belt to a shoulder. He took their sheathed Winchesters from the gunrack and, on an afterthought, helped himself to three boxes of the right calibre cartridges from the ledge below the rack. Before unlocking the safe, he hurried to the window for a quick appraisal of the Main Street scene. The gun-thunder wasn't abating, riders still careering back and forth, locals trading shots with them. He found the key that opened the safe, retrieved and pocketed his and Stretch's combined bankroll, then gathered up their saddlebags and packrolls. Thus laden, he hustled into the cell-block again and down to the rear door where his companions waited, three of them bug-eyed with apprehension. To those three he issued terse instructions in their native tongue.

'You will harness the team to the wagon. This you will do very quickly, but very carefully. If you waste my time with foolish questions or arguments, you will wish I had handed you over to El Capitan's cutthroats. Is this understood?'

This was clearly understood, as indicated by the alacrity with which Mapache, Bobo and Pepi scampered to the corral. Followed by Homer and Stretch, the latter strapping on his matched .45's, Larry strode to the side gate to try other keys on the padlock. His sidearms secure and his holster-thongs tied, Stretch performed the feat of leaping to the top of the fence and drawing himself up for a quick scan of the alley beyond.

'Looks clear right now,' he reported, dropping beside Homer.

'Bueno,' grunted Larry, as he unlocked the gate. 'You go with Homer while he fetches what he needs for fixin' the Gatling. By the time you get back, I'll have our horses saddled.'

'Ready, Homer?' asked Stretch.

'Remember,' stressed Larry. 'We need Homer alive and healthy. A bad-wounded gunsmith is damn near as useless as a dead gunsmith.'

'Ain't that the truth,' Stretch agreed.

'Lord Almighty,' breathed Homer, his ears ringing from the din of shooting.

'Get goin' now,' urged Larry.

'C'mon, Homer ol' buddy,' ordered the taller Texan. 'Time's a'wastin'.'

# 3

## Away and Running

When Larry shut the gate behind them, Stretch and the gunsmith moved fast down the alley. The uproar from the main street, the drumming of hooves mingled with the booming of six-guns and the sharp barking of rifles, indicated the battle of Rodriguez had reached its climax. Stretch, heedless of those ominous sounds, kept his eyes busy watching all he could see of the alley.

They reached the back door of a double-storied building, not exactly the most impressive in town.

'This is it,' offered Homer, as he tried the knob. 'And wouldn't you guess? Locked, damn it. And I got no key.'

'Move clear,' said Stretch, drawing his lefhand Colt.

With the roar of the report, the lock was shattered. Homer leaned against the door. It swung inward and he moved over the threshold mumbling, 'I'll need just a couple minutes.'

From the doorway, Stretch continued to watch the alley. At the end of the block, where a narrow laneway crossed the alley at a right angle, he briefly glimpsed an elderly townman hustling three tiny children to safety. He had one by the hand, another clinging to his back and the smallest child in the crook of his other arm. They crossed Stretch's line of vision and were lost from view and his mood was bitter. He was rememberisng Inagua and the innocents who had died there. Here in Rodriguez, would there be as many casualties — killed, wounded, maimed?

'Your couple minutes're almost up,' he growled over his shoulder.

He heard Homer's unintelligible mumbling, and then the gunsmith was rejoining him, hefting his box of tools of trade, the all-important manual folded and stuffed into his pants-belt.

'Not so much noise now,' he remarked. 'Seems to be less shootin'.'

'They ain't quit yet, so move careful,' advised Stretch, as they started back toward the jailyard. 'If I say 'down', that means you just flop, savvy? Don't talk. Don't think. Don't do nothin' but flop on your face.'

'Leavin' you to protect me,' sighed Homer.

'That's what I'm here for,' growled Stretch.

They were 20 yards from the gunsmithery when Stretch was alerted by hoofbeats close at hand. He darted a glance over his shoulder, saw the two sombreroed, gun-brandishing riders charging their mounts toward them and promptly drew his other Colt.

'Down!'

Homer went to ground with a thud as, whooping like booze-blind Indians, the bandidos began shooting. A slug sped past Stretch's left shoulder.

Another kicked up dust at his feet, and then he was crouching, elbows steadied against his hips, both Colts booming. The first rider loosed a yell of agony and back-somersaulted over his horse's rump. For the second, death would not be as sudden. His horse reared, turning on its hind hooves as, shoved off-balance by the impact of Stretch's bullet, he went down with one boot caught in stirrup. The horse sped down the alley, dragging him, and the screams chilled Homer's blood.

'On your feet and *move!*' ordered Stretch.

They ran onward, made it to the side gate and entered the jailyard to find the team in harness and the sorrel and pinto saddled and ready. Mapache and Pepi were on the wagon seat, Bobo peering between them from the forward flaps of the canopy. Larry was opening the rear gate and pantomining instructions. Homer hurried to the wagon to clamber over the tailgate. Stretch got mounted, took the sorrel's rein and yelled to Mapache.

'Okay, get 'em goin'! Vamos!'

Mapache kicked off the brake and flicked the team with his reins. The four strong-backed animals leaned against harness and began the turn toward the gateway. There, Larry warily surveyed the area beyond, a broad road bordered by some of the better residences of the town, those fine homes barely visible in the billowing dust. The raiders were moving out now, headed southward along this road and along Main.

'Got what they came for,' he guessed.

The banks, he supposed. Coin and greenbacks, American dollars, more dinero to finance a would-be despot's dream of power. He raised a hand, signaling the wagon-driver to stall the Conestoga just inside the gateway. Stretch paused beside him, asking, 'They headed out?'

'Makin' for Mexico,' opined Larry.

'Sure won't be hard to follow, the

kind of trail they're leavin',' said Stretch.

'I don't care how long it takes,' growled Larry, as he swung astride his sorrel. 'Just so long as — when we run 'em to ground — that Gatling's ready for action.'

'Sheriff'll be ready for action,' warned Stretch, 'when he finds we've all flown the coop.'

'It'll be safe enough now,' decided Larry. The dust was wafting away, the sounds of many hoofbeats receding southward. 'All right. Time to go.'

He signaled Mapache and nudged the sorrel to movement. Riding stirrup-to-stirrup, the Texans led the wagon to the road and turned right. With the dust of the retreating raiders moving steadily toward the southern horizon, he deemed it advisable to move at speed. He gave the command. Mapache yelled to the team and, soon, they were putting Rodriguez behind them, clearing the outskirts.

Squatting by the tailgate, the gunsmith

turned a deaf ear to the excited babbling of Bobo and his compadres and his eyes northward. Would they be pursued? He thought it unlikely their escape would be discovered within the next quarter-hour. Still, Gus Hines would venture into Main Street upon reviving, no doubt about that. With no more gunshots to intimidate him, the pudgy deputy would regain his nerve, probably offer Marlowe his own highly-colored account of the breakout. And would Marlowe swear in a posse to hunt them?

'Not likely,' he mused. 'He'll have bigger worries on his mind. Compared to what the raidin' party did to Rodriguez, what we did is scarce worth frettin' about.'

At noon, reaching the north bank of a narrow creek, Larry ordered a halt. The horses needed resting. Curtly, he ordered the Mexicans to unfasten the water-barrel.

'No way of guessin' how far to the next water,' he remarked to Stretch, as they hunkered by the water's edge, refilling their canteens.

'Here's where they forded,' offered Stretch. 'As if you ain't noticed.'

'Big outfit,' reflected Larry, studying the hoof-marked terrain beyond the south bank. 'Must've been better'n half a hundred.'

'Maybe so,' agreed Stretch. 'But all them Rodriguez citizens couldn't miss what they was shootin' at. There'll be dead bandidos in Main Street.'

Homer joined them by the bank in time to hear Larry's grim rejoinder.

'This sonofabitch Carrizo don't care how many men he loses. Plenty where they came from. Plenty gun-totin' trash in Sonora and Chihuahua who'll throw in with him. Right now, Carrizo's the mucho grand patron, the big boss too smart for the Federales to run down. To every other bandido, he's a hero. So they'll rally to him.'

'That's how it goes, I guess,' muttered Homer. 'You'd know, wouldn't you? You've sure had the experience.'

'There'll always be Carrizos,' Larry said bitterly.

'The trick is to settle their hash muy pronto,' suggested Stretch. 'Before too many good folks get butchered. Best time for fixin' Carrizo was right when he was gettin' started in the bandido business. Too bad we didn't run into him then.'

'He's responsible for a lot of deaths,' declared Homer. 'Both sides of the border.'

'So,' shrugged Larry. 'We ain't gonna argue about what we got to do, right? It'll be a mighty nervy chore, but somebody's got to handle it — somebody has to put Carrizo down for good and all.'

'When we nightcamp,' promised Homer, 'I'll start workin' on the Gatling.'

From the meagre supply of provisions in the Texans' saddle-bags, they rustled up an austere meal. It was not yet 1 p.m. when they forded the creek and pressed on southward.

★ ★ ★

In front of a looted Rodriguez bank, one of the town's doctors, the ageing Aaron Crotty, covered a dead man's face and surrendered him to the volunteer stretcher-bearers. He rose to trade stares with the sheriff and the tight-faced Deputy Dodson.

'I wouldn't count on it,' he muttered.

'Wouldn't count on what, Doc?' Marlowe asked wearily.

'Organizing a posse to chase those bandits,' said Crotty. 'You can forget it, Cyrus. They suffered casualties, but they're still too many, too large a force of gunmen for a party of civilians to go up against.'

'Tell me something I don't already know,' sighed Marlowe.

'You tallied 'em yet, Doc?' asked Dodson. 'Our dead?'

'Too early,' said the medico. 'Ask me later. At this point, I can only account for seven dead and as many wounded.' He named victims while lighting a cigar with trembling hands. 'Old Jed Skinner died of a gunshot-wound or drowning. I lifted his body from a water trough. Impact of the bullet drove him into the trough — face down. Young Georgie Newman will be on crutches the rest of his life, if he survives removal of a bullet from his back. Dan Stratton's wife was run down, trampled to death by Carrizo riders. Six months pregnant. I guess she couldn't move fast enough to get clear. Dan's out of his mind with grief and shock. Lucas Harper is another new widower. Matt Smith died of his wounds just now. You want to hear more?'

Marlowe shook his head. Crotty trudged away to attend other casualties and, for a few more moments, the lawmen studied Main Street. Most of the dead had been carried away. The wounded, those still conscious, feebly beckoned the over-worked doctors and their helpers. Broken glass littered the sidewalks. The managers of the local banks were holding an impromptu conference in front of the 1st National. The attack had been savage, the carnage harrowing. Over the next 24 hours, the undertakers of Rodriguez would be as busy as the doctors.

'It couldn't have happened on the day the local ranchers pay their hired hands,' scowled Dodson. 'Or payday for the mine workers at San Juan Ridge. That would've meant more men in town, the kind who'd have helped make a real fight of it.'

'We've done as much as we could do,' muttered the sheriff. 'I have a bottle of fine bourbon locked in my desk. Come on, Burl. We could both use a drink.'

'Couple times there,' said Dodson, as they dawdled toward the office, 'I thought I'd had my last shot of whiskey. On the hotel porch, tradin' shots with Carrizo's scum . . .'

'This wasn't our day to die,' shrugged Marlowe. 'I know how you feel, Burl. I felt the wind of more than one bullet.'

'When a slug comes that close . . . ' breathed Dodson.

'Yes,' said Marlowe. 'A grim reminder that no man lives forever.'

The office window was still open and had escaped damage, except for the gouged from the ledge by the bullet that had demoralized Hines. They tried the door. Dodson grimaced.

'Gus locked himself in.'

'What else could he do?' retorted Marlowe. 'He was responsible for the prisoners — and our armory.'

'As if Carrizo's scum are short of weapons,' sneered Dodson.

They had to wait for Hines to raise the bar and open up. Into the office they trudged, remarking on the condition of Hines' face. There were livid bruises on his brow and cheek-bone; his nose and one ear were bloody.

'Them damn bandido bastards!' he blustered. 'I locked up, but they come in through the window and — and beat up on me! And they turned our prisoners loose!'

Sadly, Marlowe glanced to the gunrack. The only weapons missing, he noted, were three Colts and two Winchesters, property of the tall Texans. He eyed Hines reproachfully.

'You always were a clumsy liar, Gus.'

'It's the truth I'm tellin' you!' protested Hines.

'Like hell,' jibed Dodson.

'If any of those bandidos had gotten in here, there wouldn't be a rifle or shotgun left on the gunrack,' said Marlowe.

'They'd never pass up such a chance,' growled Dodson.

'Tell it again, Gus,' ordered Marlowe. 'And, this time, let's have the truth.'

'It wasn't my fault,' groaned Hines, slumping into a chair. 'It was that Lawrence feller. I got too close to the cell-door and . . .'

'What were you doin' in the jailhouse?' challenged Dodson.

'Them three greasers was loco from fear, caterwaulin', raisin' a racket,' mumbled Hines. 'I went in to — uh — to calm 'em.'

'Just what did Lawrence do?' asked Marlowe.

'Last thing I remember, he grabbed at me and pulled me against the bars,' said Hines. 'Oh, hell! My head . . . !'

'If it had a brain in it, you'd never have gotten close enough for him to get a hand on you,' Dodson said sourly.

'He tricked me, damn him!' wailed Hines. 'And, by the time I got up off that floor, they was all gone!'

'All of them?' frowned Marlowe. 'Not just the Texans? Homer and the Mexicans as well?' He gestured to Dodson. 'Take a look.' The senior deputy hustled into the cellblock. Tired-eyed, Marlowe seated himself at his desk. Unlocking a drawer and fumbling for bottle and glasses, he worked by feel, keeping his eyes on Hines. 'Your keys were on your belt, so it was easy for Lawrence. And their horses were stabled in the jailhouse yard. From the moment Lawrence got his hand to your keys, they were set for an easy getaway.' He set the bottle and glasses on the desk and pulled the cork. 'A diversion was all Lawrence needed. And he sure had *that*.'

Returning to the office, Dodson tossed a ring of keys to Hines.

'Yours,' he said scathingly. 'I found 'em in the yard — the empty yard.'

'You mean . . . ?' began Marlowe.

'Not my idea of a fast vehicle for a getaway, but they took it just the same,' muttered Dodson, perching on a corner of the desk.

'The Conestoga?' frowned Marlowe.

'And its cargo,' nodded Dodson, as he accepted a brimming glass. He took a stiff swig of bourbon and grinned mirthlessly. 'My hunch is the Mexicans took the wagon. So damn scared, they didn't think to unload it. Just hitched the team and vamoosed.'

'I guess you're right,' mused the sheriff. 'I can't imagine a couple gunhawks like Lawrence and Woodville traveling with those fool Mexicans. But

I'm wondering about Homer. Could he be riding double with Lawrence or his partner? Doesn't seem likely *he'd* stay with the Mexicans.'

'About Homer, I'll make you a prediction,' offered Dodson. 'We'll never see him again. I hear tell his wife's gonna get herself a divorce, and . . . '

'That'll be a break for Homer,' interjected Marlowe, who wasn't feeling charitable at this time. 'He won't try to stop her. Not if he knows what's good for him.'

'Exactly what I was gonna say,' drawled Dodson. 'Wherever he's runnin', he'll keep right on runnin' till he's far from Rodriguez and that damn harpy.'

'Maybe Gledhill and the greasers ain't important,' scowled Hines. 'But them Texans — it sticks in my craw — the idea of them ridin' free. It was them robbed that Lawson City bank.' He eyed Dodson belligerently. 'I'll bet a month's pay it was them.'

'Speaking of cash . . . ' Marlowe savored another mouthful of whiskey and stared hard at the office safe. 'Check it, Burl.'

Dodson produced his keys and unlocked the safe.

'Only items missin' are what belonged to Lawrence and Woodville,' he reported. 'Their bankroll, jack-knives, whatever they had in their pockets.' He made another discovery when he turned to the shelf under the gunrack. 'And some of our ammunition. Three boxes of shells, calibre forty-four-forty.'

'Them bullets'll end up in the bellies or backs of bank cashiers, mark my words,' declared Hines.

'What d'you say, Cy?' prodded Dodson. 'I should go after 'em? I could depute maybe a half-dozen good men.'

'You couldn't persuade *one* Rodriguez man to leave town today,' Marlowe gloomily assured him. 'So don't travel far on your own, Burl. Just far enough to cut their sign, so we'll know which way they're headed and which law offices we should telegraph.'

'What telegraph?' grouched Dodson, taking a rifle from the rack, starting for the door. 'Haven't you heard? Carrizo's men cut the wires, wrecked the Western Union office too.'

He was gone less than an hour. When he returned, Hines directed him to the Jiminez Road funeral parlor to which the sheriff had been summoned by the mayor to help identify locals slain in the raid. Marlowe and the mayor were emerging when he reined up by the hitchrail. The three traded greetings, the skinny and forlorn Morty Finn remarking, 'A black day for our town, my friends.'

'Mayor Finn, you said that before,' Marlowe gently reminded him. 'Seven times, I think.'

'So many dead, cut down in their prime,' lamented Finn. 'Every bank looted. I tell you, Cyrus, it'll be many a long month before our economy recovers.'

'Nobody's apt to forget this day,' nodded Marlowe. 'Headed back to my office now, Mister Mayor. If you need me again, that's where you'll find me.'

The deputy dismounted and, leading his animal by its rein, kept pace with his chief. They returned to Main and moved on toward the law office, Marlowe listening intently to Dodson's report.

'The wagon and both riders — heading south you say? Burl, that's not logical.' He shook his head perplexedly. 'They took advantage of the upheaval and broke jail. *That's* logical, sure. But after all the carnage and destruction caused by the raiders, why would they make their getaway in that direction? Why risk their lives? Why, if they were sighted by Carrizo's scouts . . . '

'It doesn't make a whole lot of sense, but it's true enough,' insisted Dodson. 'I checked, made certain-sure. After they quit by way of the rear gate, they made for Cortinez Road and swung south. Ground's all broke — all the way to the south end of town. Must've been a sizeable bunch of Carrizo riders rode out that way . . . '

'That's how it was,' nodded Marlowe. 'They left by Main and Cortinez.'

'But the wagon-tracks showed clear,' Dodson assured him. 'Looked like the Texans led 'em out. And, when they turned, they sure as hell turned right — meanin' south.'

'Homer Gledhill's a peacable man,' remarked the sheriff. 'By now, if he's in that wagon or sharing a horse with one of those Texans, he is also a very worried man. Apprehensive. In fear for his life.'

At 4 o'clock, a great many locals waxed wistful upon sighting blue-uniformed riders entering Main Street from the north. There were only six, an officer, a noncom and four troopers, the latter leading horses rigged to carry packs.

'Why couldn't it be your whole outfit ridin' in,' an old man called to them.

'And why couldn't you have got here this mornin'?'

'Around ten o'clock,' scowled another local. 'In time to give us protection.

By the time the cavalrymen were reining up in front of McLeannan's General Mercantile, Mayor Finn was on hand to greet them and begin a heated but accurate account of the raid. The officer expressed his regrets and agreed it was tragic that Company A of the 2nd Cavalry was camped too far north to be alerted by the din of gunfire in Rodriguez.

'You're angry, sir, and with good cause,' he conceded. 'I'm disappointed and acutely embarrassed — also with good cause.'

'Don't be rough on the captain, Mister Mayor,' chided the noncom, a scrawny, weatherbeaten, thick-mustached sergeant. 'Wasn't any way we could know what was happenin' here. If the captain had his way, this outfit would've fought and licked El Capitan's hellions long before now.'

The captain, some 10 years his sergeant's junior, winced in exasperation and muttered a reprimand.

'As officer commanding A Company, it's *my* prerogative to deal with civil authorities.'

'Why couldn't your outfit be garrisoned right here in Rodriguez?' challenged the mayor. 'Confound it, Captain, this raid brought our town to its knees. If we're attacked again . . . '

'That's not likely, Mayor Finn,' said the captain. 'Lightning and El Capitan rarely strike in the same place a second time. And, besides, I'm under orders.'

'Well, see here now,' suggested Finn. 'While your men're loading your supplies, why don't we get together with the county sheriff and talk this thing over? You're gonna need a full report anyway, aren't you? Tell you what. Sheriff's office is down that way.' He pointed. 'You head down there and I'll fetch a bottle and be right with you.'

'We're on duty, Mayor Finn,' the captain said sternly.

'Fetch the bottle anyway,' urged the noncom.

'Sergeant Corrigan!' scowled the captain.

'Captain?' grinned the sergeant.

'Forget it,' sighed the captain.

In Marlowe's headquarters, a few minutes later, the officer and sergeant were formally presented by the mayor.

'Captain Nathan Burke, Sheriff,' offered the officer. 'I would prefer to add 'at your service'. However . . . '

'We're under orders,' nodded the sergeant.

'Sergeant Thomas Corrigan,' Burke said curtly. 'Who may soon become *Corporal* Corrigan.'

While the mayor played barkeep, the military and civilian authorities discussed the latest outrage perpetrated by the Mexican wolf-pack. Mayor Finn and Sheriff Marlowe went into grim detail about the Rodriguez raid. Captain Burke offered the assurance that the 2nd Cavalry would continue its efforts to seek and destroy El Capitan's band. He would, of course, lead the company under his command in a run to the border in hopes of apprehending the raiders on American ground.

'It should be remembered, however, that the United States government cannot risk a breach of international law,' he warned. 'Were I to pursue the bandits into their homeland, the consequences could be disastrous. I and every man under my command would face court martial. We cannot — dare not — engage this enemy anywhere south of the border.'

'Well,' shrugged Marlowe, 'I guess that's understood.'

Burke sampled another mouthful, nodded genially and remarked, 'It must be some small comfort to you, Sheriff Marlowe, that your headquarters escaped damage in the raid.'

'I'm grateful for that,' nodded Marlowe.

'But we don't much appreciate the breakout,' growled Dodson.

'Breakout?' frowned Burke.

'Our prisoners took advantage of the general upheaval,' said Marlowe. 'One of them overpowered the only deputy on duty and borrowed his keys.'

'Lawrence tricked me,' scowled Hines.

'How many got away?' asked the sergeant.

'All six of 'em,' complained Dodson. 'It was too easy for those smart-aleck Texans, Lawrence and Woodville. Their horses and saddles were in the jailyard, the team-animals too and the Gatling stolen from Mesa Valdez . . . '

'That Gatling was recovered?' demanded Burke.

He listened incredulously to the sheriff's account of the attempted stage hold-up and the capture of Mapache, Pepi and Bobo.

'And now they're on the loose again?' frowned Corrigan. 'They still got the Gatling and the ammunition — and the wagon they used for sneakin' it away from Mesa Valdez?'

'Headed south — can you beat

that?' muttered Dodson. 'If I thought Lawrence and Woodville and Gledhill were loco, I could believe they're taggin' the raidin' party. Those Texans were strangers hereabouts, but Homer Gledhill's a local — or was.'

'What were they in for — these Texans?' asked Corrigan.

'Really, Sergeant, the sheriff's escaped prisoners are of little importance in this terrible outrage,' Burke said irascibly. 'You should show more concern for the theft of an army Gatling gun.'

'I don't know what they can do with it, since it can't be operated,' shrugged Marlowe. With a whimsical grin, he suggested, 'Maybe those three raggletail Mexicans formed an attachment to it, couldn't bear to be separated from their prize. No offence, Captain, but it was quite a coup, don't you agree — their purloining a Gatling from an army post?'

'On Fourth of July,' Burke reminded him.

'I was askin' what those Texans were

arrested for,' prodded Corrigan.

'They robbed a bank at Lawson City,' declared Hines. 'I recognized 'em right here in Rodriguez from the description we got from Lawson.'

'The bank robbers were uncommon tall,' explained Dodson. 'A thief can disguise himself, but can't do much about his height, you know? Lawrence now, he'd be six foot three or thereabouts. As for his partner, hell!'

'Woodville has to be six and a half feet,' opined Marlowe. 'Not an inch less. I've never seen a man so tall.'

'You get a confession from 'em?' enquired Corrigan.

'They tried to fool us,' said Hines. 'Claimed they rode northeast from some two-bit town in Sonora.'

'Inagua, they called it,' said Dodson. 'Carrizo gang came a raidin' while they were there — they said.'

'They're a cool pair,' remarked Marlowe. 'As well as retrieving their bankroll and weapons, they helped themselves to three boxes of shells for their Winchesters.'

Abruptly, Burke finished is drink and consulted his watch.

'Thank you for your hospitality. Mayor Finn and Sheriff Marlowe,' he said courteously. 'But we've no more time for socializing — I'm sure you understand.' Corrigan rose with him and, side by side, they were a study in contrast, the sergeant so scrawny, gnarled, deliberately informal, the captain a paragon of military virtues, spruce, handsome, well-barbered, straight-backed, every inch the professional cavalry officer. 'The packhorses will be loaded by now, so we must return to our bivouac, order A Company to saddle and resume our search for El Capitan's marauders.'

'Good hunting,' the mayor said fervently.

'I forgot to ask . . . ' began Corrigan, following his captain to the doorway.

'More questions?' challenged Burke.

'I savvy how the three Mexicanos were brought in and you told me about Lawrence and Woodville,' said Corrigan, his curious eyes on the deputies. 'But what about this other runaway — what's his name? Gledhill?'

'He was in for wife-beatin',' offered Hines.

'Just a hard-workin' gunsmith who couldn't take any more naggin' from his wife.' Dodson grinned and winked. 'And his mother-in-law.'

'That ain't wife-beatin',' opined Corrigan. 'That's self-defense.'

'Sergeant!' barked the captain.

On their way back to the McLennan emporium, he chided the noncom — an old and privileged acquaintance — for badgering the local lawmen with his questions.

'Important questions,' retorted Corrigan. 'This is one of those times, Captain sir, when I know more than you know.'

'That's *most* of the time,' complained Burke,' in your opinion.'

'*I* didn't say that,' leered Corrigan, '*You* did.'

'You are the most insolent, irritating

97

sergeant in the entire Second Cavalry,' chided Burke.

'Whatever you say,' shrugged Corrigan. 'But, while we're headed back to camp, I'm gonna tell you a thing or two and, if you're smart, you'll lend an ear.'

# 4

## The Daggetts of Arkansas

Captain Nathan Burke was glad to turn his back on Rodriguez, a town mourning its dead, a devastated community, a grim reminder that, for many months, the army had hunted bandidos in vain. El Capitan's raiders continued to elude the cavalry and preyed at will on poorly defended settlements north of the border. He was bedeviled by the resentment and indignation typical of military men eager to engage a hard-to-find enemy.

A half-mile from Rodriguez, with the troopers and pack-animals at their rear and out of earshot, he strove to thrust all thought of the bandit-pack from his mind, at least temporarily, by rebuking Sergeant Corrigan for his informality.

'I pity other officers who owe

their lives to a roughneck noncom, a hooligan wearing three stripes,' he grouched. 'Damn it, Corrigan, you take too many liberties. You are far too presumptious. Certain standards must be maintained. That, Sergeant, is the army way, as you should well realize.'

'I know just how you feel,' drawled Corrigan. 'A year ago, when an Apache arrow had you down, one leg pinned to the ground, three Apaches headed for you — swinging tomahawks — I should've saluted before I shot two of 'em and sent the other runnin'. And, come to think of it, you had a musket ball stuck 'tween your ribs. That was mighty presumptious of me. I'm plumb ashamed of how I dug that slug out of you rightaway — 'stead of waitin' for Surgeon Major Halliday to get through doctorin' five other casualties. Wouldn't be fair for me to remind you that slug had to come out — fast — else maybe you'd have got blood-poison.'

'All right . . . ' sighed Burke.

'Gettin' that arrow out of your leg was quite a chore,' Corrigan went on relentlessly. 'But I must've done it right, huh? Well, I mean, you're still walkin' around on that leg.'

'*All right* . . . !' Burke growled through clenched teeth. 'Confound your Irish insolence. You've certainly made your point.'

'Burke,' mused Corrigan. 'Might that be a Swede name? Dutch maybe? French . . . ?'

'Enough!' scowled Burke.

'Okay if I talk now?' asked Corrigan.

'You defy all my efforts to silence you,' muttered Burke. 'And now, I presume you intend explaining your keen interest in Sheriff Marlowe's missing prisoners?'

'Lawrence and Woodville, ever hear of 'em?' asked Corrigan.

'Never,' said Burke.

'They only used their genuine given names,' said Corrigan. 'I oughtn't expect officers to remember 'em, but maybe you'll recall their family

101

names — Valentine and Emerson?'

'Vaguely,' frowned Burke. 'I believe I once heard talk of a couple of Texans, with scant respect for the army or for any civil authority. They were described as trouble-shooters, if my memory serves me . . .'

'That's them,' nodded Corrigan. 'I'd bet my pension they're the same two jaspers flew the Rodriguez coop. No jail could hold 'em, once they set their minds to gettin' the hell out.'

'You fought in the Northern Army in the war.'

'First Illinois Volunteers.'

'Yet you express admiration for Valentine and his companion, who are probably veterans of the Confederate Army.'

'Sure enough, they were Southern cavalry, and sure I admire 'em. It's what they've been doin' *since* the war. That's what I admire. You ain't heard?'

'Only wild rumors.'

'Wild nothin'. Most of it's true. Every newspaper writer can't be lyin',

Captain. Why, them trouble-shooters have fought and beat more outlaws than you could keep tally of. And they're still alive and healthy — and plenty smart.'

Burke sniffed disdainfully.

'This, Sergeant, is beginning to sound like hero-worship.'

'I'm a soldier that likes winners,' declared Corrigan, 'even winners that ain't soldiers any more.'

'So, nowadays, the intrepid Valentine and Emerson are soldiers in mufti,' Burke said boredly. 'Their new enemies are the lawless of the frontier.'

'That's about the size of it,' nodded Corrigan.

'You are irritating me again,' chided Burke. 'And that's a sure sign you're about to take the liberty of advising me.'

'Right,' said Corrigan. 'I'm advisin' you that our best chance of runnin' El Capitan's killers to ground is to take A Company to the south of Rodriguez and . . . '

'Find and follow the tracks cut by the raiding party,' said Burke. 'May I remind you I've already made that decision?'

'Find and follow track of the Texans — and the wagon,' countered Corrigan.

The captain slanted an incredulous glance at him.

'Is it your belief Valentine and Emerson are actually hunting those bandits, just the two of them, with three Mexican sneak-thieves and a wife-beater?'

'A wife-beater who happens to be a gunsmith,' grinned Corrigan. 'Think about that, Captain sir. How do we know how bad that Gatling's damaged? How do we know it ain't some little — uh — . . . ?'

'Malfunction? Minor defect?'

'You took the words right out of my not-so-educated mouth. Some little gadget Gledhill could easily set to rights. If he can do that, they're in business, don't you see?'

'Are you saying . . . ?'

'I'm sayin' one Gatling can raise as much hell as a whole company of fast shootin' carbines. With that Gatling operational, by golly, they'd have an edge on the whole Carrizo outfit. Valentine's alive and healthy, but most of the scum him and Emerson have fought are in prison or fillin' six-foot holes. Don't that mean anything to you? Hell! It means Valentine's as cunning as he ever was — else him and his partner'd be as dead as their enemies.'

'What you're suggesting is distasteful to me,' muttered the captain. 'I should assume those roughneck gunmen will actually locate El Capitan's secret hideaway? I should follow them at a respectful distance, leading my troopers? I should wait for them to engage the bandits, then take advantage of the havoc caused by the Gatling — always supposing Gledhill can get it working?'

'I sure admire the way you read my mind,' Corrigan said admirably. 'That was real smart, Captain sir. Now you see why you're a captain and I'm just a . . .'

'You are incorrigible and intolerable!' snapped Burke.

He subjected the sergeant to a severe tongue-lashing. Nevertheless, by sundown A Company was quitting the bivouac and moving south.

* * *

It was after sundown when the Texans sighted a flicker of light somewhere within the stand of trees 90 yards left of their route. Until now, they were agreed it was past time they nightcamped, both of them disgruntled at having failed to find a suitable site.

'Time enough later,' growled Larry, signaling Mapache to halt the team.

'Damn right,' agreed Stretch. 'If there's any clear ground inside that timber, it'd suit us fine. But it looks like somebody got there before us. So — the next thing we got to do is . . .'

'Uh huh,' nodded Larry. 'Find out who's camped there.'

'Bandidos?' suggested Stretch.

'Quien sabe?' shrugged Larry. 'We'll take a look.'

They moved back to the wagon to alert Homer and the jumpy Mexicans. Larry unsheathed his Winchester and passed it to the gunsmith.

'Just in case,' he muttered.

'Well, all right,' sighed Homer. 'But, if you hear this rifle talkin', you better get back here fast. I'm remindin' you I haven't yet had a chance to check this Gatling.'

The terrain between the trail of the bandidos and the stand of timber was thick-grassed, muffling the hoofbeats of the sorrel and pinto, and still the Texans advanced cautiously. At the near edge of the timber, they dismounted, ground-reined their horses and prepared to proceed on foot, Larry with his right fist full of cocked Colt, Stretch with his rifle at the ready.

Through the trees they crept, their

goal the dancing firelight.

'I don't hear nobody,' Stretch said softly.

'No traveler lights a fire and leaves it,' countered Larry. 'Not in country as dry as New Mexico. Somebody's there. They just ain't talkin'.'

They advanced all the way to a spacious clearing and came to a halt, saddened by the scene before them. Larry lowered the hammer on his Colt and holstered it. Stretch dipped the muzzle of his Winchester. The rig visible beyond the fire was a sorry sight, a ramshackle, pitiful two-wheeled vehicle. Once two-wheeled. Only one wheel showed now. At the near side, the end of an axle was almost a foot deep in the earth. A furrow extended from it to the far edge of the clearing. Closer, away to the right of the Texans, a man and a girl toiled beside the carcass of a horse, the man scrawny and stooped and grey-bearded, wielding a typical farm tool, a mattock, the young girl, small but strong and willing, looking to be no more than 18; she pitched in while sobbing, spading earth from the hole as fast as the man broke it.

'That's a grave they're diggin',' observed Stretch. He swallowed a lump in his throat. 'Ain't that the damnedest, most pathetic thing you ever saw? Looks like the old horse hauled 'em a ways after they busted a wheel — then just flopped and died.'

'We'll talk gentle to 'em,' decided Larry, as they broke cover. 'They've had trouble enough without us spookin' 'em.' He called to the couple. 'Rest yourselves! We'll be glad to relieve you of that chore!'

They jerked to a halt. The man had dropped the matlock and taken up a Sharps rifle — very quickly. Just as quickly, the freckled, auburn-haired girl let go of the spade and reached to her belt. She wore a jacket that hung to her hips, a flat-crowned wreck of a hat and moleskin pants tucked into boots that had seen better days. From her belt, she tugged a Colt with a 4¾ inch barrel. The hammer was thumbed back and the muzzle aimed at Larry's chest. At once, the tall man spread their arms.

'Make like your frozen sudden,' the man commanded them. His face was grey-stubbled and deeply lined, his eyes dark, moody, but alert. 'Name yourselves and tell what you're doin' here.'

'He's Emerson, I'm Valentine,' offered Larry. 'When we get friendlier — meanin' after you quit pointin' them guns at us — you can call him Stretch and me Larry. What we're doin' here is lookin' for a campin' place. We saw your light and . . .'

'And we came snoopin' careful,' declared Stretch.

'Pa and me is leery of snoopers,' the girl said grimly.

'Well, we had to snoop, had to play it safe,' Stretch said defensively. 'How'd we know it wasn't bandidos camped here — less we came and snooped?'

110

'Bandidos?' challenged the man.

'You're gonna call us liars.' Larry grinned placatingly. 'But the plain truth is we're trailin' most of El Capitan's bunch. That's a whole army of Mex killers you likely never heard of, if you're strangers in this territory.'

The man's face contorted but, to their relief, he lowered his rifle.

'Think I never heard of El Capitan, huh?' he challenged.

'Well, you ain't local,' opined Larry.

'Ain't Texan neither,' said Stretch. 'But you sure are Southern folks.'

'We're the last of the Daggetts of Arkansas,' the man told them. 'These past couple years, we was homesteadin' a right likely piece of bottom land 'bout fifty mile northeast of here. Seven weeks ago, a whole pack of El Capitan's sonosabitches raided my farm just for the hell of it.'

'Stompin' our crops, settin' fire to our barn,' murmured the girl. 'Shot the milk-cow — even the hogs and the chickens.'

'I tried to hold 'em off from a window,' growled the farmer. 'Scored on one of 'em. And him I'll know when I see him again.'

'Anybody hurt?' asked Larry.

The Texans had joined the Daggetts by the half-dug grave. Larry offered his Durham.

'What do we call you?' asked Stretch.

'I'm Moses Daggett. This here's my daughter Verna — only kin I got left.' He shook his head to Larry's offer, squatted on the piled earth and fished out corncob and tobacco pouch. 'Wasn't no bullets hit us, but all that whoppin' and shootin' was too much for my Ruby. Her heart was weak. She — just died — with her head in Verna's lap.'

'Your wife,' guessed Larry. 'Moses — Verna — I'm sure sorry.'

'Man couldn't crave a better woman,' mumbled Moses. He filled and lit his pipe and eyed the tall man moodily. 'Dunno if we'll ever go back to the homestead, Verna and me. Depends.'

'On . . . ?' prodded Larry, hunkering beside him.

'On what's gonna happen after we find them raiders,' scowled Moses.

'We'll find 'em, Pa,' Verna said encouragingly. 'You just know it.'

'Think we're crazy, don't you?' Moses challenged the Texans. 'One old Arkansas dirt-farmer and his girl-child, just the two of us cravin' to fight that many bandits? Well, hear me good! There ain't gonna be no peace for us. We don't sleep easy. Never gonna feel right — about anything — till we kill us some of them stinkin' scum. And if it means the death of us, we'll die happy. Just so long as we take some of 'em with us.'

'Ma dead,' breathed the girl. 'Critters butchered. Only animal they missed was old Jimbo.'

'Loaded the old rig and hitched old Jimbo,' said Moses. 'All we loaded was grub for us and feed for the horses. I sold a few things for just enough cash to buy my girl a pistol — so she could do her share when the time came.'

The Texans traded sober glances.

'We don't think you're crazy, Moses,' muttered Larry.

'Wheel busted, huh?' frowned Stretch.

'A ways back,' nodded Moses. 'We got out and durned if Jimbo didn't keep on haulin' till his strength gave out. Got us to here. Then he just — kinda nickered at me — and flopped and died.'

'He was real old, but the only critter we had for pullin' the rig,' sighed Verna.

'Had him since he was a two-year-old,' Moses said dejectedly. 'And, by damn, he was too good a friend to leave for the wolves and the buzzards. So we plan on buryin' him decent.'

'Yeah, well, you're through diggin',' said Larry. 'There's a half-dozen of us.'

'Includin' three puny, no-account Mexicans,' drawled Stretch. 'They ain't good for much, but they'll take their turn diggin'. Don't spook when you see 'em, Verna honey. They never rode with El Capitan — never could.'

'If they're so no-account, how come you let 'em travel with you?' demanded Moses.

'We got a wagon and a good strong team — four horses,' explained Larry. 'They ain't so useless they can't drive the wagon.' He had built a cigarette. From the fire he took a twig and got his quirley working. 'Moses, we better make a deal. I can't leave you and Verna afoot, not in this kind of country, so you're welcome to throw in with us. You crave to fight El Capitan and so do we. Stretch shot us near a dozen jackrabbits after we started out, so we'll eat hearty tonight.'

'Us Daggett's ain't lookin' for charity,' frowned Moses.

'Ain't offerin' charity,' said Larry. 'You got oats in that old rig? We got us a team, but no feed for 'em. So what d'you say?'

'Don't seem like we got much choice,' reflected Moses. 'Not if we're fixin' to catch up with them killers.'

'Just one other thing we better agree on,' warned Larry. 'This kind of huntin' party can't have but one leader — and you're lookin' at him.'

'Well . . . ' began Moses.

'That don't mean I'd have to boss you around,' Larry suggested. 'Easier if we all work together, huh Moses?'

'Pa, it's another chance for us,' Verna said eagerly. 'At least we'd be movin' again. And there'll be eight of us. Eight can do a whole lot more shootin' than just two.'

'You know why I gotta find them kill-crazy polecats,' said Moses. 'What's *your* reason?'

'There's fat bounty on El Capitan,' drawled Larry. 'But we got a better reason than money. We were in two towns that got raided by El Capitan's men, one in Sonora, the other a ways north of here. What we saw — well — that's all the reason we need.'

'Well . . . ' The farmer nodded slowly. 'Seems like we all got the same idea.'

'Fetch the others,' Larry urged Stretch. 'We'll help with the buryin' and nightcamp here.'

'I reckon it'll be safe enough,' remarked Stretch. 'At least we got men enough to post guards all night long.'

'Right,' nodded Larry. 'No Carrizo scouts'll catch us sleepin'.'

The wagon and saddle-horses were brought to the clearing. Larry introduced Homer and the Mexicans and briefly explained the Daggetts' situation, then put Mapache and his buddies to work. That scruffy trio completed the chore of burying the horse, a mite intimidated by the grief and fury of the Arkansas man, lost in admiration for his daughter, but not yet mustering the courage to compete for her favors.

Over supper, Homer spoke his mind to the farmer.

'Maybe this won't make much sense to you, friend, but you got plenty to be thankful for — compared to me.'

'I buried my Ruby on land trampled by El Capitan's scum,' said Moses, eyeing him morosely. 'And I should be thankful?'

'Compared to me,' Homer emphasized.

'How come?' demanded Moses.

'Your Ruby was a lovin' woman,' the gunsmith pointed out. 'Made you happy, bore you a right fine little girl-child. So you got good memories, somethin' worth recallin'.'

'Uh huh,' grunted Moses. 'That's the truth.'

'My Theodora's a mean one,' confided Homer. 'Used to give me hell from sun-up to sundown. Never bore me any children and, soon enough, her mother moved in with us, so I had two of 'em plaguin' me all the time.'

Moses digested that along with a mouthful of jackrabbit stew, then conceded, 'I don't reckon I could've stood for that. Never had such trouble with my Ruby.'

'I stood it too long,' sighed Homer. 'And — when I couldn't take it any more — I kind of lost my head . . . '

He dared to confess his ungentlemanly

reaction to the last tirade inflicted on him by Haughty Hester and daughter, causing Moses to gag on another mouthful. When he finishes coughing and caught his breath, the farmer surveyed him disapprovingly.

'No man oughta do *that*.'

'You don't know Theodora,' countered Homer. 'Or her mother.'

'So that's why you quit Rodriguez — scared off by a couple of women?' challenged Moses.

'Well, not exactly,' frowned Homer. 'Plain truth is I got thrown in jail after Theodora swore a charge against me and said as how she was gonna get a divorce. And, when El Capitan's renegades raided Rodrizguez, Lawrence decided the county jail was no safe place for us. So he busted us out.'

'You're all jailbirds?' gasped Moses.

From the other side of the fire, Larry drawled a reassurance.

'Don't be frettin' about the company you're keepin', Moses. My partner and me didn't do what they arrested us

for. And Homer sure ain't dangerous.'
He grinned genially at the gunsmith.
' 'Cept to naggin' women.'

'And we are caballeros, senor,' leered
Mapache.

'When the fighting begins, we will
protect the senorita,' promised Pepi,
aiming a grin at Verna.

'You will, huh?' growled Moses.
'Well now, I'll tell you somethin',
little feller. If my Verna ever has to
protect herself against you, there'll be
three more graves to be dug.' He eyed
the Mexcians warningly. 'Just your size.
Know what I mean?'

'Hey, Mapache, nobody trusts us,'
whined Bobo.

'We will have their trust,' bragged
Mapache. 'Ah, si! Also the respect of
these gringos — when we show our
courage in battle!'

Supper ended, Larry ruled the
Daggetts and the Mexicans should
call it a day; it might be necessary
to rouse one of them in the early
hours to take a turn at standing watch.

He would patrol the timberline until relieved by his partner. And, by the light of an oil-lamp provided by Verna, Homer would make his first inspection of the most important item inside the wagon.

'Time for you to switch your stuff to the big rig,' he told Moses. 'There'll be room aplenty.'

It was then, while passing sacks of oats over the tailgate of the Conestoga, that Moses and daughter stared into its lamplit interior and saw the Gatling for the first time, Homer tinkering with its firing mechanism. Moses frowned from the Gatling to the stacked belts of ammunition, then back to Homer.

'Heard of them there big guns,' he muttered. 'Never ever seen one before. Used a few in the war, didn't they? But not in any battle my old regiment mixed into.'

'This model will fire better'n two hundred rounds a minute,' Homer told him. 'It's on tripods, see? And not so heavy it can't be toted. Weighs a mite under a hundred pounds. If I can fix it, Moses, and if we can find El Capitan's camp — well — we might do what we started out to do.'

The farmer smiled for the first time in a long time, a cold, mirthless smile. To his wide-eyed daughter, he remarked, 'It'll be worth throwin' in with a bunch of jailbirds.'

Around 10 o'clock, while the others slept, Homer descended from the wagon and quit the clearing to seek Larry. He found that wide-awake, alert-eyed veteran nursing his Winchester at the west fringe of the timber, surveying the moonlit terrain north and south.

'Any luck, Homer?'

'By lamplight, you can only do so much,' said Homer. yawning. 'I'll be at it again come sun-up. Plan on rolling the tarp back, give me more light.'

'So what d'you think?' demanded Larry.

'I can do it — I can get it workin',' muttered Homer. 'Found what caused the trouble. Last soldier tried to use it, he forgot what he was taught, didn't rig it right before he started turnin' that handle. Soldier-boys . . . ' He shrugged impatiently. 'What do *they* know?'

'Manana?' asked Larry. 'Before we move out?'

'You want to test it?' offered Homer. 'I could show you how.'

'No need,' Larry said casually. 'This won't be the first time Stretch and me worked a Gatling.'

Homer was taken aback.

'Honest?'

'A while back,' nodded Larry; for just a moment, grim memories came to mind. 'Place called Mesa Rico. Won't talk of it now. Too long a story.'

'All right,' said Homer. 'After breakfast maybe.' He frowned worriedly. 'And that reminds me. How're we fixed for provisions? Eight mouths to feed now, don't forget.'

'You know of any settlements 'tween here and the border?' asked Larry.

'I can remember Castejon,' said Homer. 'Traveled down there a year and a half ago. Good enough town. Not as big as Rodriguez. They don't have a gunsmith. I had to collect and repair some rifles, as I recall. Let's see now . . . ' He stared away to the south. 'Yeah. Sometime tomorrow, if tracks of the bandidos keeps us movin' straight south, we'd pass right close to Castejon. But what do we use for cash for provisions?'

'We got plenty,' said Larry. 'I wasn't about to leave our bankroll in the sheriff's safe. Not so you'd notice. Go on back now. Homer. Get your sleep so you'll be clear-headed and bright-eyed come sun'up.'

'When *you* sleep?' demanded Homer.

'Couple more hours and I'll rouse Stretch,' said Larry. 'I figure he'll last till maybe four o'clock. Then Moses or one of them Mexicanos can take over.'

Homer returned to the clearing in time to witness a scene that caused him anger and amusement, in that order. The anger began when he spotted one of the Mexican's, Bobo, furtively crawling to the blanket-covered bundle that was the apparently sleeping Verna. Bobo had almost reached her and the gunsmith was about to bellow a scatching reprimand, when the girl's eyes opened. Bobo's swarthy face was less than 12 inches from hers. He paused, grinning. She showed him a bland smile and the muzzle of her gleaming, brand-new Colt. His grin faded. Not a word was said and now Homer's anger gave way to amusement. Bobo crawling backwards to his sleeping place resembled a prairie dog in slow and awkward retreat.

Verna tucked her gunfilled hand under her blanket, aimed a cheery smile at the broad-grinning gunsmith and went back to sleep. While bedding down near the wagon, he found himself envying the Arkansas man. How different it might have been, had Theordora born him a daughter of the calibre of little Verna.

At midnight, Larry trudged to where

his partner lay snoring and nudged him with a boot. Stretch jack-knifed from his blankets, traded nods with Larry and, after donning his Stetson and taking up his rifle, loafed away to take his turn at guard duty.

The taller Texan returned, yawning wearily, around 4.15 a.m. Moses was stirring by then, so he offered his Winchester to the farmer, who rose up and, with a blanket draped about his shoulders, trudged to the timberline.

Breakfast was meagre, but the Mexicans discreetly refrained from grouching. The atmosphere brightened a little when Larry announced his intention of arranging purchase of provisions from the settlement of Castejon this day. Homer did his eating while working on the Gatling with the wagon's canvas canopy rolled back. A little while later, while Verna was gathering dishes and her father kicking dirt onto the fire, the gunsmith replaced his tools in his box along with the manual and called to Larry.

'Ready for testin'.'

'Bueno,' nodded Larry. 'Stretch, help Homer lift it down. Mapache, you and your buddies scout the timberline, keep your eyes peeled for travelers. Better if nobody else hears this devil-gun workin'.'

While the Mexicans scanned the terrain surrounding the timber, the Gatling was hefted from the Conestoga by Homer and the taller Texan. A belt of ammunition was in position. Larry crouched behind that fearsome weapon, directing it to the first line of trees on the south side of the clearing. He rolled and lit his after-breakfast cigarette and waited patiently for the Mexicans to return. The Daggetts, after a last sad appraisal of their empty, useless vehicle, kept their eyes on Larry and the Gatling. A few minutes later, Mapache and his cronies rejoined them to report the area to all sides was devoid of any sign of life.

'So go ahead, runt,' urged Stretch. 'I already pegged Homer for a right smart gunsmith, but you might's well make sure.'

Larry worked his cigarette to the left side of his mouth, took hold of the firing handle and squinted through the sight. He gave the handle just three turns. The saddle and team horses flinched to the chugging sound and the profoundly impressed onlookers watched the effect on the trees, suddenly pitted and gouged by the hardhitting .65 calibre rounds.

Loath to demonstrate further, determined to conserve ammunition, Larry ceased firing; he was satisfied.

'Good, steady action, huh?' grinned Homer.

'Any bandidos that don't surrender,' drawled Stretch, 'They'll sure wish they had.'

'Let's load 'er aboard, spread that tarp and get rollin',' said Larry.

Fifteen minutes later, back on the trail scored by the southbound raiders, Moses and his daughter were relishing the experience of traveling in a durable, dependable vehicle drawn by a sturdy team. He had elected to drive. Verna shared the seat with him and traded friendly talk with the taller Texan on the smart-stepping pinto keeping pace with the rig. In back, Homer squatted by the Gatling, his eyes turned north, while the Mexicans hunkered behind the forward seat, making tentative efforts to include themselves in the conversation between Verna and Stretch. Larry chose to ride some 30 yards ahead, studying the broken ground and the terrain all the way to the southern horizon.

They saw no game that morning. Pausing only to rest their animals, they drank water sparingly and looked to Homer who, after scanning the land to the east, reassured them.

'It's startin' to look familiar. Couple more hours on this route and we ought to sight Castejon's smoke about a hundred yards over thataway. And, unless it dried up, there'll be a waterhole.'

At 2.10 p.m. they came to the waterhole and sighted, away to their left, the rising smoke and the rooftops of the settlement dominated by a church steeple.

'That's Castejon,' nodded Homer. 'Right neat little town — unless it was hit by a raidin' party.'

'You're about to find out,' Larry told the gunsmith. 'I'd send Stretch to fetch our supplies, but that'd be a bad mistake.'

'There you go again,' scowled Stretch.

'Any time I let you travel off alone . . . ' began Larry.

'You got to humiliate me in front of these folks?' grouched Stretch.

'Well,' jeered Larry. 'Pardon me all to hell.'

'Whose saddle do I borrow?' asked Homer.

'Both,' said Stretch, and the Texans dismounted. 'Takin' an extra horse, you get to fetch extra grub, maybe enough to hold us till — uh — till we're through travelin'.'

'Please, Pa . . . !' began Verna, dropping from the wagon.

Moses frowned down at her.

'Now what?'

'It wouldn't cost more'n a few cents,' she pleaded. 'And I ain't had nothin' like that in the longest time.'

'You know durn well we got no cash — not a dime,' he chided.

Larry, passing money to Homer, frowned curiously at the farmer.

'What's she talkin' about, Moses?'

'Soap,' Moses said impatiently.

'Real soap that smells purty,' the girl murmured. 'I scarce ever had any. And, next time I get to take an all-over bath . . . '

'Well, what the heck, Moses?' shrugged Larry. 'It don't much matter about us, but women're different. We oughtn't forget Verna is female.'

'*I* will *never* forget the senorita is . . . !' began Bobo.

'Shuddup,' growled Stretch.

'Us Daggetts ain't lookin' for handouts,' protested Moses.

'Aw, c'mon, Moses,' wheedled Stretch.

'You'd have plenty to cuss about if I wanted to buy her hard liquor or jewels to turn her purty head — or a silk gown or such,' Larry conceded. 'But a little soap to make her smell good — feel good? Where's the harm?'

'Well . . . ' shrugged Moses.

'And can I ride in with Mister Gledhill — can I?' she begged. 'Then I can choose my own soap!'

Moses gave his consent and, a few minutes later, straddling Larry's sorrel, Verna was riding stirrup-to-stirrup with the gunsmith, bound for Castejon and a harsh reminder of the raid on the Daggett homestead.

# 5

## Scarred Face and Dun Horse

Cassius Rodd, town marshall of Castejon, was another expatriate Texan. Despite his age, the unruly hair visible under his battered Stetson showed no grey; Castejon folk had given up on trying to guess the number of his years. The face was weathered and deeply lined, his grey eyes shrewd and observant, the physique devoid of excess fat and the memory unfailingly dependable. He kept it that way, his memory, by exercising it regularly.

Sharing the porch of Rodd's office when the elderly man and the shabbily-garbed girl rode past was an old crony, Walter Harbridge, owner of two local livery stables. He puffed on a bent-stemmed brier while Rodd gnawed on a cold cigar and identified one of the passing riders.

'Be all of eighteen months since he last stopped by. Didn't get to meet him, but I can name him.'

'Braggin' again,' Harbridge good-humoredly chided.

'Gledhill,' said Rodd. 'Comes from — uh — Rodriguez. Yup. Rodriguez. Runs a gunsmithery up there.'

'And the girl?' demanded Harbridge.

'Never saw her before,' drawled the marshal, slumping lower in his caneback chair, letting his Stetson slant over his eyes. 'But I'll remember her if I see her again.'

'You and your memory,' muttered the stableowner. 'Too bad you've never seen any of El Capitan's scouts. Then you could ease my mind about those gun-hung vaqueros been pussy footin' around town this past hour.'

'Never saw them before,' said Rodd. 'Maybe they're vaqueros visitin' from some Chihuahua Rancho and maybe they're bandido spies, here to size up Mayor Culbert's bank. I'll decide, Walt.'

'When?' frowned Harbridge.

'When I get around to it,' said Rodd.

'And when'll that be?' asked Harbridge.

'When they make their first wrong move,' said Rodd.

Verna's mood was cheerful. Oblivious to the disapproving stares of the matrons of Castejon, startled by her unconventional attire, she dismounted with Homer in front of a general store and followed him inside.

'All right now, have your fun,' he invited. 'Take your pick of all the fancy soap while I'm doin' business.' He nodded affably to the storekeeper. ' 'Afternoon. My friends and I are short on provisions.'

The storekeeper began transferring canned goods from his shelves to the counter and proved himself an astute salesman.

'Got canned peaches too, okay? Fine. Eight cans. Listen, friend, I couldn't help noticing. No offence, but that's no way for the little lady to pack a pistol. Belt and holster'd be safer.'

'Don't know if I have cash enough,' frowned Homer.

'I could make you a good deal on a cartridge-belt and holster,' offered the storekeeper. 'Shave my price a little? You don't have to decide till I've filled your order.'

After inspecting all the soap on display, Verna fetched a wrapped cake to the counter. Homer sniffed at it, flashed her an indulgent grin and urged her make it two more cakes.

'No so expensive, kid, and Lawrence won't mind.'

Larry had provided more than enough cash for their needs. With her precious soap stowed in the pockets of her jacket, the delighted Verna strapped on the gunbelt. The obliging storekeeper used a bodkin to dig an extra hole, the better for her to secure it about her slim waist. The Colt fitted snugly into the holster. Then, while the men began packing the provisions into sacks, the girl wandered to the street window for another appraisal of the merchandise on display.

By chance, she glanced beyond the window display to the street and, hitched to a rail opposite, saw the four horses, all wearing Mexican saddles. One of those animals she studied with her heartbeat quickening, a dun colt. In dismay, she shifted her gaze to the two well-armed Mexicanos lounging on the sidewalk. Homer and the storekeeper were starting for the entrance, each hefting a bulging sack, when she saw a third Mexican amble into view and address the other two briefly. His face was turned her way for a fleeting moment and she felt her gorge rise. The jagged scar running from cheekbone to chin of that swarthy visage was frighteningly familiar to her.

Pausing in the doorway, Homer eyed her sidelong.

'You sick or somethin', kid?'

'No — no — I feel fine,' she mumbled. 'We — goin' back to camp now, Mister Gledhill?'

'Rightaway,' he nodded. 'Got to remember there are six hungry men waitin' for this stuff.'

She followed the men out, watched them secure the provisions to the horses, then remounted the sorrel. The storekeeper bade them farewell and withdrew. And then, as Homer raised a boot to stirrup, the girl spoke to him softly, urgently.

'Don't let on, Mister Gledhill. Do it casual.'

He frowned at her.

'Do what?'

'There's Mexicans — other side of the street. Look at 'em so you'll know 'em again. But — but they mustn't guess you're interested.'

Impressed by her demeanor, the gunsmith obeyed her command with great discretion. He removed his hat and, while mopping his brow with his kerchief, threw a casual glance to the hitch-rail, the four horses and the seemingly indolent Mexicans. Then he finished mounting.

They began a slow exit from Castejon by way of an alley angling west off the main street. Quietly, he asked, 'What was that all bout?'

'Don't tell Pa,' she begged. 'Better you tell Mister Lawrence. But please don't tell Pa. He'd load up his old Sharps and come a 'running' and — maybe get killed.'

'You're sayin' those Mexicans were in the raidin' party — when your mother died?' he demanded.

'Dunno about the other two, but I'm dead sure about the one Pa wounded, his with the scar,' she murmured. 'Pa don't know I saw him. I didn't know Ma was gonna die. Thought she just fainted. It was when I crawled to the crack in the door and snuck a look that I saw him hit by Pa's bullet — him with the scar. And he was ridin' the dun. Near fell off of it.'

'You got a good look at his face, huh?' he prodded. 'No mistake? Same man?'

'It's him for sure,' she insisted.

'And — oh, Uncle Homer, I near threw up when I saw him!'

The 'Uncle Homer' touched his heart. Awkwardly, he reached sideways to pat her trembling shoulder.

'Now you try and forget it, hear? Want to leave it to me to talk to Lawrence about it? Sure you do.'

She asked nervously,

'What — what d'you suppose Mister Lawrence'll do?'

'Don't you fret,' he soothed. 'Whatever he does, he'll do it right.'

How long would the Carrizo men remain in Castejon? Homer asked himself that question when they returned to the camp by the waterhole. And, with no way of answering it, he deemed it wise to parley with the Texans at once.

They talked out of earshot of the Daggetts and the Mexicans while the provisions were loaded into the wagon bed, all but what they would need for a substantial meal; already, Verna was opening cans.

The Texans stayed poker-faced

while the gunsmith repeated everything confided to him by the girl. Predictably, Stretch left the decision-making to his partner.

'Just what're we gonna do about this, runt?'

'I won't know what *I'm* gonna do till I ride to Castejon with Homer,' muttered Larry. 'But I know what *you're* gonna do. You're gonna stay put — and stay sharp. Any Mexicans come by while we're gone, be ready for anything, savvy? Any bastard makes a hostile move, don't give him any kind of chance.'

'You want me to ride back with you?' frowned Homer.

'You've seen 'em,' Larry reminded him. 'I haven't.'

Stretch deftly transferred his lefthand Colt to Homer's waistband. Homer winced, but only for a moment.

'All right,' he nodded. 'Ready when you are — trouble-shooter.'

Moses and Mapache waxed curious when Larry and the gunsmith swung astride the sorrell and pinto. With a wry grin, Larry remarked,

'I must be gettin' old. Can you imagine me sendin' Homer for supplies — and forgettin' to have him fetch us some whiskey?'

'For shame, runt,' jibed Stretch.

'You folks go ahead and eat,' urged Larry, as he nudged his mount to movement. 'I ain't sure how soon we'll get back.'

Homer's nerves were a'clamor as, with Larry at his side, he rode to Castejon again. This was more than he had bargained for when agreeing to throw in with the living legends, the distinct possibility of joining one of them in violent action so soon after quitting Rodriguez. He worked hard at controlling himself and refrained from questioning his impassive companion.

Reaching the main street, they slowed the horses to a walk and approached a saloon a short distance from where the scarred man and his cohorts still lounged.

'That's them?' asked Larry.

'That's them,' grunted Homer.

'So we tie up at the saloon,' decided Larry. He passed money to the gunsmith. 'You buy the booze and stow it in the saddlebags while I watch and wait.'

'You mind tellin' me exactly what you're waiting' for?'

'Four critters at that hitchrail, Homer. Only three men. I should settle for three when, if I wait patient, I could nail all four of 'em?'

'I think I'm sorry I asked,' sighed Homer.

They dismounted at the saloon hitchrail and looped their reins. Homer disappeared into the saloon. Larry, unhurriedly building a smoke, advanced a few paces south along the plank sidewalk and squatted on a bench to covertly study the Mexicans. He gave them his full attention, never guessing he too was under observation.

The town marshall of Castejon had quit the porch of his office some little time ago. Now, he was in a barber-shop a few doors from the store patronized by Homer and Verna earlier, but not for a haircut or shave. While the barber worked on a customer, Rodd stood at the street window, a knowing grin creasing his leathery visage, his shrewd eyes on the seated stranger. To the consternation of the barber, he drew and checked his sidearm, a handgun heftier than most, a conversion Colt Dragoon. The barber had regarded it as a somewhat unwieldy weapon until some six months ago, when the marshall had drawn it to discourage a likkered-up cowpoke from taking pot-shots at the flagpole atop the town hall. The alacrity with which the Dragoon had cleared leather, cocked and leveled at the rowdy, left a lasting impression on every onlooker, including the barber. Re-holstering the weapon, Rodd resumed his vigil.

Homer emerged from the saloon to pack wrapped bottles into the saddlebags of the Texans' horses, then sidled to the sidewalk bench to squat beside Larry.

'I wonder how long . . . ?' he began.

'This'll be him,' opined Larry.

As well as studying the Mexicans, he had appraised the four horses, a dun, a calico, a charcoal and an appaloosa; these bandidos liked variety, or maybe it was just a happy coincidence their animals were so distinctive. The fourth Mexican was tall for a Mexican, all of six feet and heavyset. He swaggered out of a bordello and, spurs jingling, moved along to join his companeros. After trading a few words with him, the scarred man and the other two rose and moved to the hitchrail.

'Now?' breathed Homer.

'Few more seconds,' muttered Larry.

'Well — what the hell're you waitin' for?'

'I need to know which sonofabitch belongs on which horse.'

'Why?'

'Later, Homer.'

Larry rose quickly as the tallest of

145

the four mounted the white pony. The saddles of the dun, the black and the appaloosa were filled with the riders about to move off when, quickly, Larry rose and stepped into the street, calling to them harshly. Rodd promptly transferred himself from the barbershop window to its doorway. Homer rose and moved a few yards closer along the sidewalk, his worried gaze on the four horsemen staring at Larry.

'You are speakin' to us, gringo?' challenged the scarred one.

'You know it, bandido,' growled Larry. 'Beats me how you Carrizo spies got the nerve to show your faces in this town. You loco? Think I don't know who you are — and why you're here? Sizin' up a bank, I bet.'

'Borrachon,' leered the tallest bandido.

'That better be the last time you call me a drunk,' Larry warned him. 'Don't give me no Mex back-talk. I savvy the lingo good.'

'We do not like to be called bandidos,' snapped the scarred man.

'We are vaqueroes of the Rancho Cortez.'

'Hogwash,' scowled Larry. 'I know you for sure. You're one of the bastards raided a farm northeast of here seven weeks ago. Your scar's a dead giveway.'

'We will listen to no more of your insults, gringo,' the tallest rider declared. 'We go now.'

'The hell you do,' countered Larry. 'You're gonna climb off of them caballos and walk to the marshal's office.'

'Well now, that sounds fair,' drawled Rodd. Larry didn't make the mistake of taking his eyes off the horsemen, as Rodd emerged from the barber shop and sauntered into the street to stand a few feet to his right. 'Saludos, senors. Just happens I'm the marshal. Name of Cass Rodd. Got to agree with this tall hombre. Cool your saddles and we'll parley — in my office.'

'We are honest vaqueros . . . !' The scarred man began again.

'My ass you are,' grinned Rodd.

'You're here to spy for your bigshot boss, the cucaracha that calls himself El Capitan. Well, this time, El Capitan don't get no information. You won't be ridin' home to talk about the Castejon bank.'

'I'm through waitin'!' growled Larry. 'If your Mexican butts ain't out of them saddles in three seconds, I'll blow 'em out!'

That grim threat goaded the four to swift and violent action. They whisked out their pistols at deadly speed but were outdrawn by Larry and the lawman. Recovering from his initial shock, Homer jerked Stretch's Colt from his pants, cocked and aimed and squeezed trigger. His bullet struck the scarred man's gun-arm and sent him hurtling from his mount.

The sudden din of booming Colts caused citizens in the next block to scatter for cover. The tallest bandido was toppling, a victim of Larry's first shot. Rodd accounted for the man on the appaloosa, putting him down with a bullet in his head. A slug skimmed the brim of the lawman's Stetson and the man on the black wasn't given a second chance. Larry's Colt roared again. The fourth man shuddered from the impact of the bullet and, pawing at his mortal wound, pitched to the dust. Wincing guiltily. Homer returned Stretch's pistol to his waistband.

The echo of the last shot of that bloody affray slowly died away. After a wary glance at the unruffled Rodd, Larry moved forward to check on the fallen. Casually, Rodd followed him. Homer moved off the sidewalk and, from downtown, another lawman came bounding onto the scene, young, wide-eyed and waving a six-gun.

'My deputy,' Rodd apologetically informed Larry. He called an order. 'Mitch, boy, stash that damn hogleg before it goes off and hurts a law-abidin' citizen!'

The young deputy holstered his gun as he jerked to a halt to gape at the sprawled bodies.

'Holy smokes, Marshal . . . !'

'You got a chore, Mitch,' drawled Rodd. 'Three of these heroes're dead as they'll ever be. You load 'em on the horses and take 'em to the planter on Santera Road. He'll be glad of the business. Mister Valentine and me gonna tote Handsome to the office.' He indicated the groaning desperado with the scarred face. 'When you get through at the funeral parlor, go tell Doc Beesley I got a patient for him.'

'Mitch . . . ' Larry called sharply to the deputy, halting him in his tracks. 'I want their duds and their hardware. And don't mix 'em up. Four bundles, savvy?' He glanced at Rodd again. 'I'll need their horses too. You called me by name. If you know who I am, you know I got my reasons.'

'Marshal . . . ?' frowned Mitchell.

'Do what the man says,' ordered Rodd.

Larry and Homer helped with the grisly chore of draping the dead over their horses. The gunsmith flinched as, while hauling the scarred man to his feet, the marshal addressed him by name.

'Good to see you again, Homer Gledhill. We didn't meet last time you came down from Rodriguez, but I never forget a face or the name that goes with it.'

'Oh?' Homer shrugged uncomfortably. 'Well — uh — howdy.'

'You and me never saw each other before,' Larry assured Rodd.

'Not in the flesh,' said Rodd, nodding affably. 'But I always had the feelin' I'd meet up with you some day.' As they moved off, he prodding the groaning prisoner, Larry keeping pace, Homer leading the horse, he eyed Larry curiously and remarked, 'One thing I don't savvy. I was just a young'un when I first heard of you, so how come you look younger'n me?'

'It's the life I live,' growled Larry. 'Quiet, easy, steady, never no strife. Keeps a man young.'

The marshal chuckled approvingly.

'You got a sense of humor.'

'Have I?' shrugged Larry. 'I never noticed.'

As the scarred man flopped to his knees, Rodd grasped him by the collar of his conchoed jacket and jerked him upright.

'On your feet, Fernando, and keep movin',' he ordered. The prisoner turned to gape at him. 'Surprised I know your name? You were so smart, you and your companeros. Hangin' around, talkin' all the time, never guessin' I got close enough to hear you. The Capitan's gonna be real disappointed, huh Fernando? This time, no message for your good-for-nothin' boss.'

They reached Rodd's office. With scant regard for his reduced condition, Fernando was shoved roughly into the four-cell calaboose. He sagged onto a cell-bunk, right arm bloody from above the elbow all the way down to the wrist.

'He's got another wound not full-healed yet,' Larry assured Rodd. He made short work of stripping the prisoner to the waist. 'Uh huh. There it is.'

Rodd frowned at the tender area at Fernando's left side.

'Raided a homestead, I heard you say.'

'Homesteader's name is Daggett,' said Larry. 'They burned his barn, butchered most of his stock and trampled his crops. He held 'em off from a window. One bastard he creased.' He eyed Fernando contemptuously. 'Scar-faced bastard on a dun horse.'

Scratching a match, Rodd revived the cold cigar jutting from the side of his mouth.

'Well now,' he drawled. 'I've had me the privilege of sharin' a shootout with a right famous pistolero. And Texan. That's the best part.' He grinned over his shoulder at the gunsmith hovering about the cell doorway. 'Ain't forgettin'

153

you, Mister Gledhill. You don't feel bad about shootin' this hombre — I hope?'

'I never shot a man before,' muttered Gledhill.

'Maybe you never had to,' retorted Rodd. He studied Larry again. 'This is what brought you to New Mexico? You got a hankerin' to settle El Capitan's hash? Listen, if anybody can do it, you're the one.'

'Wherever he holes up, I'll find him,' declared Larry. He spoke clearly and watched Fernando's reaction. 'His killers headed south after the Rodriguez raid. Left plenty sign. Taggin' that many riders is no hard chore.'

'Loco gringo!' gasped the scarred man. 'From the rim, the guards will shoot to kill! You will not live to see the cuartel general!'

'Don't bet on that, Fernando,' drawled Larry.

A local doctor arrived with the young deputy in tow. Rodd nodded for him to attend the prisoner and told the deputy,

'You stay with 'em. He's hurt too bad to try for a break, but watch him anyway.'

Mitch McKenley's eyebrows shot up and the doctor frowned impatiently, as Larry unceremoniously divested the prisoner of outer clothing. He then followed Rodd back to his office to dump the commandeered clothing beside the three neat piles delivered by Mitch, each pile topped by coiled gunbelt and sombrero. While Rodd checked the coffeepot on the Justin stove, he moved to the open doorway a moment to study the four horses at the hitchrail. Homer, suddenly weak at the knees, suffered a delayed reaction, discreetly found a chair and took the load off his feet.

'Their clothes, weapons and horses — I can use 'em,' Larry told Rodd.

'Use some coffee too?' asked Rodd, rummaging for extra cups. 'I could improve the taste and give it a little muscle. Got most of a pint of sourmash around here someplace.'

'Nobody's gonna object,' said Larry.

While pouring coffee and boosting it from a whiskey bottle, Rodd offered his official attitude to the death of three Carrizo men and the capture of one.

'The law had to take its course, Valentine. You identified one of 'em and, anyway, I never had no doubt they were spy-bandidos. They had their chance to surrender peaceable, so I got no call to hold you or Mister Gledhill. But, about their horses and duds and stuff, you better tell me why you want 'em.' He passed a cup to Larry, another to Homer and raised the third in cheerful toast. 'Here's perdition to El Capitan and all his kind. Texas forever and remember the Alamo.' They drank to that. Then, 'You can talk free to me,' he assured Larry. 'And I can keep Mitch's mouth buttoned tight.'

'My partner and the sodbuster, Daggett and three others are camped a little ways east,' said Larry. 'Some of us are of a size with Fernando and his gravebait companeros. Straddling their animals and rigged in their duds, I figure there's an even chance we'll get close enough to Carrizo's guards to draw their teeth. You heard Fernando shoot off his mouth. Guards at the rim of the cuartel general, he said.'

'And I savvy enough Spanish to read his meanin',' nodded Rodd. 'Rim of a sizeable basin, I'd guess. Cuartel general means headquarters. So five'll get you ten he was talkin' of El Capitan's hangout. Likely yonder of the border, somewheres in Chihuahua. But we don't know that for a fact. Might be this side of the line.'

'Do I get what I've asked for?' demanded Larry.

The lawman moved behind his desk and seated himself. They sipped reinforced coffee and traded stares.

'Valentine, I've been a friend of yours many a long year, though you didn't know it,' Rodd said quietly. 'I know there are plenty badge-toters crazy-jealous of the way you and Emerson work, all the owlhoot scum you've nailed — and always fightin' to your own rules. Bein' Texan-born, I was never jealous, never hankered to turn a key on you. So I'm an old friend and admirer, you understand?'

'Bueno,' grinned Larry. 'You can call me Larry.'

'I'm Cass to my friends,' said Rodd. 'And I care about my friends, you know? Don't like to know a friend of mine is gonna play hero and maybe bite off more'n he can chaw. Seven of you, huh? Four of you rigged as bandidos to fool the guards. Uh huh. Sounds good. And, if it works, you get to the rim of a basin where the Carrizo gang's camped. But what happens *then*? You're seven against an army of bandidos. Why should I let you take what you want — knowin' this could mean the end of the Lone Star Hellions and their five sidekicks? Is that how I should treat a friend?

Larry swallowed another mouthful and frowned pensively.

'Think we should tell him?' he asked Homer.

'Your decision,' shrugged Homer.

'He carries a badge,' Larry pointed out.

'But calls himself your friend,' said Homer.

'Question is,' mused Larry, 'would it be fair, me dealin' him in on our secret? We're his guests right now. Guests oughtn't put their host in a spot — after partakin' of his hospitality.'

'A secret?' frowned Rodd. 'Listen, first I'm a Texan, *then* I'm the marshal. The Texan's givin' his word — one Texan to another — he'll keep his mouth shut.'

'You won't get all riled up?' prodded Larry.

'I can be one mighty cool hombre,' Rodd reminded him. 'You saw how I faced up to them Carrizo gunhawks.'

'All right,' said Larry. 'We got a Gatling.'

'Oh, sure!' Rodd chuckled good-humoredly. 'And I got a half-dozen

159

cannon in the yard out back. Like to have a little extra fire-power around in case Mexico declares war on the States. You and your sense of humor, Larry. You sure enjoy a joke.' Abruptly, he waxed serious, apprehensive too. 'You *are* jokin', huh? You couldn't — hell, no — you *couldn't* be huntin' El Capitan with a Gatling!'

'Beats rifles and handguns,' shrugged Larry, 'When you're outnumbered.'

Rodd's jaw sagged.

'How in blazes could this be? I mean, damn it, you don't stop by the corner store and buy a doggone Gatling!'

'Somebody borrowed it,' Larry said off-handedly. 'From some army post.'

'Mesa Valdez!' breathed Rodd. 'I got a bulletin from the Second Cavalry commandant. It was non-operational and it disappeared Fourth of July.'

'It works fine now,' said Larry.

Rodd's shocked gaze switched to Homer, who winced apologetically and downed the rest of his spiked coffee at one gulp.

'You're a gunsmith,' accused Rodd. 'You could do it!'

'Could and did,' said Larry.

'Stolen army ordnance,' protested Rodd.

'Well, I'll tell you — old friend,' drawled Larry. 'My sidekicks and me, we ain't the kind who'd want to keep — uh — a gun that ain't ours. We plan on returnin' it to the army after we're through usin' it. Why, sure. They'll get it back — 'cept for the ammunition we throw at Carrizo's army.'

'You wouldn't go back on your word, would you, Marshal?' asked Homer.

Rodd fretted a moment longer. He eyed Larry reproachfully until the itching of his funny-bone forced him to grin again.

'I got only one regret,' he confessed. 'As town marshal, my authority extends no farther than the limits of the settlement of Castejon. That means I can't ride with you.'

'We've got men enough anyway,' opined Larry. 'The Gatling'll make a heap of difference.'

'I guess you already thought of this,' said Rodd. 'If you can do it, the Mexican and United States governments'll be powerful grateful — and the Second Cavalry'll never forgive you.'

'That grieves me,' Larry assured him with a crooked grin. 'Sure hate to hurt anybody's feelin's. Only party I want to hurt is Ricardo Carrizo. And as many of his killers as get in our way.'

'Take everything you want and welcome,' urged Rodd. 'And, if you get out of this ruck us alive and thirsty, come back to Castejon and let's celebrate.'

# 6

## Last Chance for Quitters

In the late afternoon, the five men and the girl rose and stared westward to follow the advance of Larry and the gunsmith, each leading two saddled but riderless horses. First to voice a reaction, Moses Daggett clenched his fists and declared,

'I could swear that's the same dun, the critter rid by the Mex that felt my bullet!'

'It's the same horse, Pa,' frowned Verna.

While Stretch and the Mexicans traded puzzled glances, the farmer frowned at his daughter.

'How could you know?'

'I know for sure,' she murmured. 'Don't have to talk about it rightaway, do we, Pa? I'll tell you later. I promise.'

'Four right purty animals,' observed Stretch. 'Saddles're kinda flashy.' He eyed Mapache sternly. 'Kinda finery you hombres'd favor.'

Moses began his questions before Larry could dismount.

'All in good time,' countered Larry, as he swung down. 'Stay patient a while, Moses. You'll get answers — when I'm good and ready.' He detached a bulging sack from his saddle and nodded encouragingly to the Mexicans. 'Fetched you some vestidos. Better than them beat-down duds you're wearin'.'

'Some right fancy hardware too,' said Homer, unslinging a sack and upending it. To the ground tumbled four pearl-butted pistols in cocho-studded holsters affixed to ornately-tooled cartridge-belts. 'Pretty slick, huh amigos?'

'Muy bello?' grinned Larry.

'Ai, chihuahua!' cried Bobo. 'Never I see such pistolas!'

'We are poor hombres,' Pepi said humbly. 'For us, they are too much.'

'Pistolas worthy of a vaquero caporal,' enthused Mapache.

It was Larry's turn to empty a sack. 'You can strap on the hardware after you've tried on your new duds,' he drawled. 'Well, not exactly new, you understand, but in great shape, boys. Oh, sure. Real fine vestidos. Nothin' but the best for three hotshots like you.'

Warmed by his amiable demeanor, the thieves grinned admiringly at the garments arranged on the grass. Larry, after a critical appraisal of Mapache, offered the bundled clothing taken from scar-faced Fernando.

'For you, amigo. And I want you to try 'em on rightaway.'

He chose another bundle, complete with boots, and nodded to the wide-eyed Bobo.

'Just right for you. And the appaloosa comes with 'em.'

The outfit once worn by the black's rider was passed to the delighted Pepi, after which the Mexicans, momentarily

165

oblivious to the redhead, began stripping.

'Not where the girl can see!' boomed Moses.

'Larry,' sighed Homer. 'You think these boys're gonna remember anything you tell 'em?'

'They'd better remember when the time comes,' Larry softly retorted. 'It could mean their lives.'

'No call to fuss, Pa,' shrugged Verna. 'How about I hide inside the wagon with that ol' devil-gun?'

'Well, all right,' growled Moses. 'But keep lookin' the other way.'

Eagerly, clumsily, the Mexicans peeled off their shabby garments and donned Larry's offerings. He then tossed them the sidearms, making sure they matched. They set their sombreros at jaunty angles, strapped on the hardware and immediately emptied the holsters and tried to twirl the gleaming pistols by their trigger-guards. Stretch and Moses made to throw themselves flat, Larry grimaced irritably and informed them.

'I unloaded them hoglegs. Pete's

sakes, you think I'd trust these jumpin' beans with loaded guns?'

Straightening up, Moses pointed to the fourth pile of clothing and said firmly,

'If you fetched them do-dads fer me, Lawrence, I thank you kindly — but no thanks. Wouldn't wear such rig if I was buck-naked and Deacon Willet's sister 'bout to catch sight of me.'

'Quit your frettin', Moses,' said Larry. 'I plan on riggin' myself in that outfit, but not till I need to.' He called to the girl. 'Hey, Verna, they're decent. You can come out now.'

Verna perched on the tailgate, her expression solemn and withdrawn as she watched the simple-minded thieves strutting in their new finery. Larry decided he wanted to see them mounted, and was as careful in directing them to their respective horses as when doling out the showy raiment. Mapache lithely swung astride the dun. Sniggering foolishly, Bobo straddled the appaloosa. Pepi, yearning to impress the only female member of the party, decided to mount the charcoal unhurriedly, gracefully.

'Saving the calico for yourself?' challenged Stretch.

'You guessed it,' nodded Larry. 'All right, you caballeros, climb off them animals and stand still so I can check you over again.' The Mexicans obeyed. He inspected them intently and pronounced himself satisfied. 'Yeah. You'll do.'

'Senor Lawrence, you have been muy generoso and I do not wish to be ungrateful,' frowned Mapache. 'But this fine blusa is wet — and darkly stained — and the chaqueta also.'

'My vestidos also is stained,' complained Pepi.

'Mine too,' nodded Bobo.

'Well, you oughtn't be too particular when you get somethin' for nothin',' shrugged Larry. 'Them marks'll dry out soon enough. It's just blood.'

'B-b-blood . . . ?' breathed Mapache.

'Como . . . ?' frowned Bobo. 'No comprendo.'

'Sangre!' groaned Pepi.

'*Sangre* . . . ?' wailed Bobo.

Their dismay was comical, but nobody laughed.

'Into the wagon again, Verna,' ordered Larry. 'They're through preenin' for you. Gonna switch to their old duds now.' As the girl withdrew into the Conestoga, he instructed the Mexicans curtly. 'Don't get them outfits mixed up. You tie everything to the horse you straddled, comprendo? Pistolas too.'

In 10 minutes, the subdued trio appeared as formerly, Verna was out of the wagon and breaking out cooking gear, preparing to rustle up an early supper. The plan, Larry decided, would be best outlined while they relaxed over their meal. But he could stall Moses no longer; the farmer's patience was worn thin.

Homer stayed with Verna and the Mexicans, while Stretch and Moses followed Larry behind the wagon, there to hunker and confer. For openers, Larry fixed a warning eye on the farmer.

'You get mad at Verna and, sure as I'm Texas-born, I'll get mad too, Moses. Don't you rant at her, hear?'

'Well, why would I . . . ?' began Moses.

'You got a brave little gal there,' declared Larry. 'Smart. Uses her head.'

'Lawrence, I'll thank you to say your piece — straight,' growled Moses.

'When she rode to Castejon with Homer, she got her soap — and somethin' she didn't count on,' muttered Larry. 'Sighted the sonofabitch you creased when that wolf-pack raided your place — the scar-faced hombre on the dun.' He went on to repeat what Homer had told him, emphasizing the girl's fear that, had her father learned the scarred man was that close, he would have reacted violently and to his own danger. 'So she told Homer and he passed me the word.'

'All right,' sighed Moses, nodding

slowly. 'So now you can tell me the rest of it.'

Stretch was shrugging resignedly as his partner recounted the events leading up to the gunfight and the aftermath, the parley with Marshal Rodd. Shrugging resignedly and grinning a knowing grin. Already, he was guessing at Larry's strategy; it would not be the first time they had resorted to such tactics.

'So that's where Fernando is,' Larry told the farmer. 'No way he's gonna break jail, not with a wide awake Texas lawman guardin' him. He's hurtin' from two wounds now, Moses, and he's gallows-bait. I wouldn't know when the circuit-judge is gonna hit Castejon, but it wouldn't surprise me if that scar-faced polecat is the first Carrizo man to be tried and hung.'

'Him for a gallows and three of 'em dead,' mused Moses. 'It don't ease the pain, but it's a start. Might be Verna and me gonna sleep easier now.' He frowned in puzzlement. 'But how come *she* knew the scarred Mex? I'll have to ask her about that.'

He put it to his daughter a short time later, squatting beside her while she prodded at the contents of the pots and skillet.

'Just didn't think to talk of it before,' she murmured. 'Ma was still alive when you went to shootin' from the window. 'Help your pa,' she said. I recall you kept a box of shells on the shelf left of the door and I crawled over there, but then I saw you already had them bullets beside of you. 'Fore I went back to Ma, I sneaked a look through the crack in the door. That's when I got a good clear look at him — 'about the time your bullet stung him. And — it was only a couple minutes later — Ma died with her head in my lap.'

He squinted into the cook-fire.

'Guess we'll always mourn her, Verna honey.'

'Guess so,' she agreed. 'Look, Pa, I couldn't tell you about seein' him in Castejon. You'd have . . . '

'Yup,' he nodded. 'I'd have rid in and likely got my head blowed off. You did right, child. I reckon Lawrence knows best. So, whatever tricks he's plannin', we all better listen good and do like he says.'

Verna dished up a fine supper but, several times during that meal, Mapache, Pepi and Bobo developed digestive problems, wincing in agitation as they swallowed half-chewed mouthfuls. Homer, still a mite shaken by his first experience of lethal gunplay, munched his food with great care and hung on Larry's every word, convinced these veteran trouble-shooters represented his only chance of surviving the ordeal in store. Verna was overawed, Stretch doggedly calm, Moses eating steadily, his eyes never leaving Larry's face.

As explained by Larry, the plan seemed simple enough, almost absurdly so. The advance on the bandido camp would be made boldly, the sorrel and pinto tied behind the wagon, Homer driving, Stretch and the Daggets concealed inside. Larry, rigged in the clothes once worn by the tallest of Carrizo's spies, would be riding the white horse accompanied by the Mexicans in their disguises. By this ruse, he hoped to advance to within handgun range of the guards before they could raise the alarm. At this point, Homer interjected a question.

'You thinkin' they'll open fire on us rightaway? I mean, as soon as they see you ain't Fernando?'

'Count on that,' Larry said bluntly. 'Now, Homer, when they show their weapons, there's two things we can do. Dive over into the wagon bed and stay low, or stay right where you are and do your damnedest with a Colt.'

'Well . . . ' The gunsmith shrugged fatalistically. 'I won't be much help hidin' behind the seat, will I?'

'Just don't crowd Stretch,' warned Larry. 'He'll be usin' two guns and needin' to get a bead on as many guards as he can see. You too, Moses.

But not you, Verna honey. You keep your purty head down and stick close to the Gatling, leave all the shootin' to us.' He stared hard at the Mexicans. 'You frijoles any use with a six-shooter?'

The girl's eyes were on them. They traded worried glances, then squared their shoulders, putting on a fine show of grit and determination. Mapache spoiled the effect when he answered Larry; his voice was high-pitched and quavery.

'We are grande pistoleros, Senor Lawrence. Magnifico. Expert!'

'Muy bien,' grinned Stretch. 'Guess I'll keep my irons holstered and leave all the shootin' to them.'

'You not have to do *that*!' gasped Bobo. 'Por favor, senor! We will not complain if you shoot also!'

'Gee,' leered Stretch. 'Thanks.'

'After we cool the guards, we'd better be ready to use the Gatling,' Larry went on. 'But we ain't gonna rush it and I ain't sure we ought to tote it out of the wagon.'

'If we move it to behind the tailgate, turn the wagon round . . . ' suggested Stretch.

'You're readin' my mind,' nodded Larry.

'Well, while ever the Gatling's in the wagon, you can move it fast if you need to,' Homer pointed out.

'And that could be real important,' opined Larry. 'I'm countin' on El Capitan bein' camped snug in a hollow, a basin. But that's all I got from his spy. I don't know how big a basin or how many trails lead out of it or how soon them bandidos'll cut and run. That's why we'd better be ready to change position, and fast.'

'We can't afford to show mercy,' growled Moses.

Larry matched stares with the farmer.

'No mercy for any armed rider comin' at us,' he said softly. 'But, Moses ol'buddy, we don't be throwin' down on any that want to surrender. There'll be no lead wasted on hombres that drop their guns and raise their paws. That's how it has to be, Homer. That's our way.'

'We've been called outlaw-fighters and trouble-shooters, Homer,' drawled Stretch. 'But nobody ever called us butchers.'

'Recollectin' what they did to my place, rememberin' Ruby in her grave . . . ' Moses bowed his head and sighed heavily. 'There's time I could forget I'm human.'

'You *are* human,' said Homer. 'Same as the rest of us.'

'And we ain't scum — like Carrizo and his men,' muttered Larry. 'We ain't about to kill just for the hell of it, Moses. We'll be makin' war. It won't get to be a massacre unless Carrizo's gunhawks are fired up on from tequila or loco-weed and don't know when to quit.'

'I'll remember I'm a man — not a damn bandit,' Moses promised.

'Okay now . . . ' Larry forked up another mouthful and cheerfully enquired, 'Anybody got any questions?'

'Si, I have a question,' mumbled Pepi. 'I think you are a guerrero, Senor Lawrence, and have fought many times. But — have you never been shot?'

'Often,' said Larry. He nodded to his partner. 'Wounded oftener than we could keep count, both of us. Bullets mostly, but we've been knifed a time or two.'

'It hurts, no?' frowned Pepi.

'It hurts,' nodded Larry.

'Ain't that the truth,' agreed Stretch.

'But the hurtin' passes,' said Larry. 'A man heals'.

'I got a question,' said Homer. 'The wagon. They'll wonder about the wagon. Four spies rode to Castejon, fetch a wagon and team back to the hideout, stranger on the seat . . .'

'One of these bavados'll start hollerin' to the guards,' decided Larry. 'How about you, Mapache? You got a big enough mouth.'

'But — what can I tell them?' frowned Mapache.

'How about . . . ?' Larry thought a moment. 'How does this sound? In your own lingo, you holler 'Hey, compadres, look what we got! We bring gringo hostages — a wagon full of gringo booze!' I reckon that'll do it. What d'you say, big feller?'

'It'll likely fool 'em,' opined Stretch. 'For long enough.'

The meal continued in pensive silence. Verna poured coffee and passed it around. And then Homer spoke his mind.

'I've been a gunsmith a long time and never had to use a gun in battle — till today. It didn't pleasure me any to see that Mex go down from my bullet. But, if I have to, I guess I can do it again. And I have to, no question about that. Just want to say — when the time comes — I'll try to be brave.'

'Ain't all gonna get out alive,' Moses sombrely predicted. 'Me, I'm ready to die fightin' them buzzards. The rest of you better be just as ready.'

179

'I plan on survivin' this thing,' declared Homer.

'Hopin' for the best is reasonable, I'll allow,' frowned Moses. 'But, when a man's time comes . . . '

'We'll be in good company, Moses,' the gunsmith pointed out. 'These two Texas bucks have survived more fights than you've had birthdays. So I'm hopin' some of their Lone Star luck'll rub off on us.'

More silence. Larry broke it by paying Verna a casual compliment.

'Real fine coffee.'

'And you sure cook good, Verna honey,' drawled Stretch.

'Gonna make some lucky hombre a great little wife some day,' said Larry.

She studied them intently.

'You just talkin' easy to make us feel safe — or are you always like this when — when you're about to risk your hides?'

'One thing we learned a long time back, Verna,' frowned Larry. 'Before the fightin', it's just no use frettin'.

Man might's well stay easy of mind.'

'Frettin' ain't gonna make no difference,' shrugged Stretch.

Neither Homer nor the farmer had heard the hoofbeats. The sound was barely audible when the Texans set their tin cups aside and got to their feet, hands on gunbutts. A rider was approaching. Verna and the other men were perplexed until, a few moments later, they too heard the hoofbeats.

'Everybody stay out,' ordered Larry. He moved around to the east side of the fire, then a few yards clear of it to avoid showing himself as a silhouette, a clear target to the horseman. Then the lone rider was emerging from the gloom and recognizable. 'Relax,' said Larry. 'Just Marshal Rodd payin' a call.'

'Gringo rurale!' Bobo mumbled to his buddies.

'I said relax,' growled Larry.

Unhurriedly, Rodd reined up in the firelight. He doffed his Stetson to Verna before dismounting. Larry performed introductions and gestured for Pepi to attend the lawman's animal. The little Mexican tethered it by the other saddle-horses and returned to the fire to squat beside Mapache and Bobo. Rodd accepted a cup of coffee, hunkered between Homer and Moses and aimed a genial grin at the taller Texan.

'Stretch, it's true what I've heard and read. You got to be the tallest fiddlefoot ever drifted out of the old Lone Star.'

'Just kept right on growin', Marshal suh,' Stretch said politely.

'Cass,' insisted Rodd. 'I'm Cass to the likes of you.'

'You got curious, huh?' challenged Larry. 'Just had to ride over and size up our little outfit?'

'And tell you what I've learned since you and Mister Gledhill quit town,' nodded Rodd. 'It could be true, and it might be useful.' He glanced to the wagon. 'Remind me to take a look at the Gatling before I head back to town.

Ain't seen one since the war. On wheels it was.'

'This one's on a tripod,' offered Homer.

'Marshal, I'm hopin' your prisoner's under tight guard,' Moses said sternly.

'Got my deputy watchin' him close,' Rodd assured him. 'Full name Fernando Montoya. He's been doctored and fed and now he's sleepin' — but I wouldn't say peaceable.'

'What've you got that might be useful?' demanded Larry.

Rodd sampled his coffee and got down to business.

'Montoya's wound was givin' him hell. To work on that arm, the doc gave him somethin' to quiet him down. Well, I wouldn't know what kind of booze he'd been drinkin' but, mixed with what Doc fed him, it started him raving. Delirium, Doc called it.'

'He say anything that made sense to you?' asked Stretch.

'Some would claim he didn't make sense at all,' frowned Rodd. 'How can

I be sure? But, just in case, I'm passin' it on.'

'What exactly?' prodded Homer.

'Two miles south of the border, the tall gringo will die,' said Rodd. 'He can follow track of the horses across the border into Chihuahua, Mexico, but only for two miles. That's what he said — over and over.' He nodded to Homer. 'It was you winged him?'

Homer shrugged self-consciously.

'Uh huh. The scarred man. He's the only one I scored on.'

'You did good,' said Rodd. 'Doc saved his arm, but, even if a jury acquitted him — which ain't likely — he'd be helpless in a gunfight. Some kind of paralysis, Doc said.' He eyed Larry expectantly. 'What d'you think? The hideout could be a couple miles across the line?'

'An outfit so big has to roost someplace,' mused Larry. 'Two miles south of the border — what I call close. Make it easy for Carrizo to send raiders into New Mexico and the

Arizona Territory.'

'Well,' said Rodd. 'I figured you'd want to know, and I sure hope it helps.'

'Muchas gracias,' said Larry.

'My pleasure,' said Rodd. He finished his coffee and got to his feet. 'Nice meetin' all you law-abidin' citizens of the United States.' He stared down at them, grinning wryly. 'Any of you stopped to think of it?'

'If you and Lawrence talked, you'll know we set our minds to it,' said Moses.

'You mean findin 'em in Mexico,' said Rodd. 'Raidin 'em in their own country. You'll be out of reach of the U.S. law and, when you get to where you're headed, the only law will be Ricardo Carrizo's.'

Followed by the Texans, the lawman ambled to the wagon to peer over the tailgate. He admired the Gatling for a long moment, his expression wistful.

'Bad surprise for Carrizo,' he muttered. 'With this kind of hardware,

185

you'll raise hell a'plenty — and maybe even get out alive.'

'Has to be done anyway,' shrugged Larry.

'One chore we just got to handle,' nodded Stretch.

Rodd eyed them searchingly.

'Can't change your ways, huh? You have to make your play — because you've seen what Carrizo's raiders do to harmless people, their own countrymen. And that's all the reason you need, isn't it?'

'I heard a feller say Carrizo craves to make himself the new presidente,' said Larry. 'Well now, I ain't Mexican. But I don't think I'd like that.'

'And I wouldn't like it neither,' growled Stretch.

'Peaceable Mexicans wouldn't like it,' opined Rodd. 'With Carrizo runnin' the country, it wouldn't be worth livin' in. Boss-bandidos with big ideas are the worst kind.' He thrust out his right hand. 'Could we say so-long this way? Might be my last chance to brag of shakin' the hands of the Texas Hell-Raisers.' They shook hands with him. He grinned and asked, 'Either of you lose any ancestors at San Antone — back in 'thirty-six?'

'Both of us,' nodded Larry.

'Me too,' said Rodd. 'So, when you start in on 'em with the Gatling — remember the Alamo?'

'You know it,' Larry said grimly.

They walked Rodd to his horse. He swung astride, flashed them a last admiring grin, wished them victory and survival and began his return to Castejon. Until he was lost from view in the darkness, they stared after him. The taller Texan thoughtfully remarked,

'I don't suppose every Texas badge-toter'd call himself a friend of ours, but I'm glad that one does.'

'For a while there, I thought he'd turn in his badge and join up with us,' confided Larry. 'And he'd have been a handy hombre at the showdown.'

'We're gonna have to lick El Capitan

and all his trash with what we got,' said Stretch.

'Yeah, sure,' agreed Larry. 'But we got the Gatling. What I call an advantage. Quite an advantage.'

By 8 p.m., two guards were posted, one a volunteer, the other not so willing; Moses and Pepi would stand a 3-hour watch and be relieved by Homer and Mapache. Inevitably, Larry and Stretch would work the graveyard shift.

Around noon of the following day, some six and a half hours after the bandit-hunters abandoned the waterhole and returned to tracking their quarry, the force led by Captain Burke and Sergeant Corrigan arrived. At the captain's signal, the two columns of troopers halted a short distance north of where Larry's party had camped, the better to permit Corrigan to read sign.

At this chore, Burke conceded the sergeant's superiority. Everything Tom Corrigan knew of trail-lore, he had learned from friendly redmen and old Indian scouts; there was little he still had to learn.

'Corporal Kepler,' Burke called to the other noncom. 'The men may consider themselves at ease. They may dismount and smoke if they wish, but there is to be no forward movement until Sergeant Corrigan has completed his scout.' He eyed Corrigan expectantly. 'How much time will you need?'

'Quien sabe?' shrugged the sergeant.

Burke grimaced.

'All right, Sergeant, I do realize we're drawing closer to the border. But — *please* — spare me your barracks-room Spanish.'

'Quien sabe?' repeated Corrigan. 'Means who knows? Old Mexican sayin'.' He added, off-handedly, 'A lot of old Mexicans say it.'

'Will you ever answer my question?' barked the captain.

'Yessir, Captain sir,' drawled Corrigan. 'I can't tell you how much time I'll need till I'm half-way through readin' sign.

Now how's about I get on with it?'

'I would be obliged,' Burke said sourly.

He paced beside his horse, puffing on a cigar, while Corrigan investigated the hoof and boot prints left by the hunters. Then, to his chagrin, the sergeant remounted and began a slow progress toward the settlement of Castejon. Angrily he called after him.

'Stay out of the saloons, Sergeant! You aren't on recreation leave!'

After travelling 40 yards towards Castejon, Corrigan wheeled his mount and returned to the waterhole, but slowly, warily avoiding well-marked tracks. Burke called a question which, in his irritating way, Corrigan pretended not to hear. West from the waterhole he rode to the trail scored by the southbound Carrizo riders. He studied sign intently and, at last, moved back to where the captain awaited him.

'Every trooper's belly's growlin',' he muttered. 'Now that I've checked all tracks, we might's well eat here, water our animals, 'fore we push on after 'em.'

'How far ahead of us are they?' demanded Burke. 'I'll settle for an educated guess — based on your long experience as an expert tracker.'

'I sure thank you for that compliment, Captain sir,' Corrigan said humbly.

'I was being sarcastic,' countered Burke.

'They broke camp early,' said Corrigan. 'I'd reckon the hour after sun-up. You want a hungry company chasin' after 'em — or do we eat?'

Burke called orders to the corporal, who relayed them to the troopers. Within the quarter-hour, A Company men were watering the horses and the midday meal cooking over several fires. A little while later, while they squatted side by side, eating from cans and swigging coffee, Corrigan reported his findings to his impatient superior.

'Here's how I read it. When they camped here yesterday, two of 'em traveled to the settlement — twice.

First time, a full-growed rider and maybe a kid. If not a kid, a mighty runty man, real lightweight. They came back and then two more headed out. Only, that second time, the lightweight didn't go along.'

'You continue to impress me with your trail-lore,' Burke said grudgingly. 'I presume your findings — as to the size of the riders — is related to the depth of the hoofprints?'

'No trick to it,' shrugged Corrigan. 'Not when you know what to look for.'

'Carry on,' sighed Burke.

'When the second pair of riders were through in Castejon and came back,' said Corrigan, 'They kind of multiplied. That time, there were a half-dozen horses.'

'Indicating they recruited four more men in Castejon?'

'I mean four more horses, Captain. I don't mean riders. If I had to swear to it, I'd say them extra horses was totin' saddles, sure, but them saddles were empty.'

'Interesting,' frowned Burke. 'And a trifle confusing.'

'Valentine and Emerson ain't horsethieves,' shrugged Corrigan.

'Perish the thought.' Burke smiled bleakly. 'They have their standards.'

'Wouldn't take me long to ride over to Castejon, maybe find out . . . ' began Corrigan.

'That won't be necessary,' Burke decided. 'We know they have resumed their pursuit of the enemy, Sergeant. For the present, that's all we need to know.' He finished his coffee, wincing in disgust. 'Will army cooks never learn to make respectable coffee . . . '

'That's your misfortune,' jibed Corrigan. 'Fine gentleman like you — used to the better things of life. Me now, I can make do because that's how I was raised. Always makin' do, makin' the most of what I got.'

Burke curtly changed the subject.

'I have consulted our map and, according to my calculations, we should reach the border in two days, perhaps less. If we find Carrizo's headquarters on the American side, it will be a stroke of luck and we'll certainly take advantage of it.'

'Be music to my ears,' enthused Corrigan, 'when you order the charge. Bugle blowin'. A Company advancin', showin' the flag . . . '

'Only if the enemy is found this side of the border,' Burke grimly emphasized. 'Remember now, Sergeant. Strict protocol will be observed and national boundaries respected. You'll never see the day when Nathan Coleridge Burke would commit such a disastrous error. To lead this company onto Mexican soil — by Godfrey — it would be unthinkable, inexcusable, flagrant disregard for all military ethics, an abandonment of correct procedure . . . '

'I guess what you're sayin' is we didn't ought to do it,' frowned Corrigan.

'I intend making that your responsibility,' declared Burke. 'And, if you value your stripes, you'll remember you're a non-commissioned officer of the United States Cavalry, not a free-roaming, trouble-shooting outlaw-fighter, not a trigger-happy civilian. Is that understood?'

'Yeah, sure,' nodded Corrigan. 'Tell me what I'm supposed to do. And I'll do my damnedest.'

'You will be our advance scout,' said Burke. 'When our map reading indicates we have reached the border region, I'll be relying on you to locate the marker. There is bound to be a marker, Sergeant. Usually a makeshift monument, a milestone, perhaps a signpost.'

'If it's there, I'll find it,' Corrigan assured him.

'You will be a half-mile ahead of us,' explained Burke. 'At the end of every half-mile, you will wait for the company to catch up before proceeding the next half-mile. I trust this instruction is clear?'

'You always give clear orders,' remarked Corrigan. 'If any big-shot officer, like a general for instance, asked me what I most admire about Captain Burke, I'd say it's the clear way he gives orders.'

'Sergeant Corrigan.'

'Sir?'

'Shut up, for pity's sake, finish your coffee and let's be on our way.'

Mobile again, A Company resumed its trailing of the people trailing the raiding party.

After sundown of that day, from the south edge of a brush-clump, Larry stared to the thickly-timbered ridge far to the south, noted the glow of four campfires atop the hogsback and decided their quarry were taking their time. This could not be El Capitan's headquarters, but no stray-hunting, peaceable ranch-hands had built those fires. He was looking at the night-camp of the band that had raided Rodriguez.

# 7

## Enemy to the Rear

In the brush, the hunting party had found enough clear ground on which to picket the horses. The wagon was almost invisible to the people resting a few yards away, thick growth crowding it from both sides. The Mexicans, always helpful where Verna was concerned, had piled dry wood for a fire. The night was still, not a breath of wind, little danger the brush would ignite. But there was to be no fire.

Larry came trudging back to them just as Homer tossed his matches to Pepi.

'Forget it,' he growled. 'Tonight, no hot grub, no coffee.'

'No fire?' frowned Stretch.

'A fire would tip our hand, and we don't want to do that,' said Larry. 'I figure we got two things workin' for us.' He hunkered closer to the group and dealt it out. 'The Gatling's the big ace up our sleeve, sure . . . '

'And what else?' demanded Moses.

'We've been trailin' 'em steady and careful,' Larry pointed out. 'Ridin' point, the beanpole and me been keepin' our eyes peeled, found no tracks of rear scouts stakin' out to check their back-trail.'

'Meanin . . . ?' prodded Homer, as he retrieved his matches.

'They ain't onto us,' said Larry.

'I'd bet on that,' offered Stretch.

'So they haven't caught on,' mused Homer. 'Don't know they're bein' followed.'

'And that's another edge we got on 'em,' nodded Larry. 'We need the Gatling, but we also need the advantage of surprise.'

'Seems like we'll have that advantage,' opined Moses.

'We will win!' bragged Mapache. 'This will be a great victory!'

He slanted a covert glance at Verna, hoping for an approving smile. She eyed him dubiously and looked away.

'Gettin' close, are we, runt?' asked Stretch. 'That why we're gonna eat cold grub?'

'You guessed it,' said Larry. 'They ain't hustlin', and that's another reason we've caught up.'

'Plenty confident, these killers,' frowned Homer.

Rising, Larry jerked a thumb.

'C'mon. You might's well see. All of you.'

He led his people to the south side of the brush and, for a while, they stood quiet, studying the four points of light on the ridge.

'How much farther?' wondered Stretch. 'Got a feelin' in your bones, runt?'

'I'm a stranger here myself,' drawled Larry. 'Mapache, what d'you say? We anywheres near the border?'

'Manana,' said Mapache. 'Si. Maybe in the last part of the morning, we will come to the pilar de anuncio.'

''Less we find Carrizo's hideaway 'fore we see the sign-post,' argued Moses.

'I wouldn't count on that,' frowned Larry. 'All along, I've been thinkin' we'll have to cross the border to get a shot at Carrizo.'

'You wouldn't try for a sneak-attack on that bunch?' asked Homer, gesturing to the ridge.

'That'd be less than half of 'em maybe.' Larry's eyes gleamed. 'Not enough, Homer. I want the whole lousy outfit.'

'So . . . ' Stretch shrugged fatalistically. 'Seems like we're gonna be visitin' Mexico. Only it won't be no sociable visit.'

'I'll sit guard here, just in case,' muttered Larry. 'Rest of you go eat.'

His companions withdrew into the brush. A few minutes later, Moses Daggett returned, toting two cans of beans and pork with forks protruding. He squatted beside Larry and, while they plied their forks, made his request. What he said was said very calmly, politely, dispassionately. The Arkansas man was very much in control now, disciplining himself. And resigned to the possibility of sudden death.

'Got a kindness to ask of you, Lawrence.'

'So ask.'

'You didn't say it, but I had the feelin' you're lookin' for it to end tomorrow.'

'Tomorrow'd be my guess.'

'I know you're no stranger to this kind of action. Homer told me what you and your partner been doin' since the war.'

'What we've been doin' is tryin' to stay peaceable, Moses. Ain't our wish it didn't work out that way.'

'Well, you got experience — and a lot of luck. Might be I won't be so lucky. Aim to follow orders and protect myself as best I can, but there could be a Mex bullet with my name on it. I can accept that. Already made my peace with the Lord. What I'm askin' is — if you get out alive and I don't — would you look out for the girl?'

'Do what we can for her, Moses.'

'Just put her on a horse and point her toward Arkansas. We got no kin there, but friends a'plenty, the kind who'd take her in.'

'I reckon we can do better than that, Moses. We'd never let her try it alone. If she has to head back to Arkansas, we'll be ridin' escort, takin' good care of her.'

'That eases my mind some,' mumbled Moses, munching on a mouthful.

'Fine,' grunted Larry. 'So how about *you* ease *my* mind some?'

'Anything I can do,' offered Moses.

'Somethin' you should *quit* doin',' growled Larry. 'A man could get killed, sure. That's somethin' we all got to allow for, but it don't mean we have to count on it. Better to figure on doin' your damnedest to survive, Moses. Keep tellin' yourself 'This'll be the death of me' and it just might, savvy? Fight hard, old timer, but defend yourself good. Cover yourself. Take no crazy chances.' He accounted for another mouthful and put a hard question. 'I'll allow it's rough for a man, losin' a good wife like Ruby. But are you so grieved you don't want to live any more?'

'There have been times,' Moses gloomily admitted. 'But — I keep rememberin' Verna.'

'Keep right on rememberin' her,' urged Larry. 'For her sake, fight hard but wary. If some Mex sharpshooter is gonna score on you, don't make it any easier for him.'

They finished eating. Moses nodded pensively and got to his feet.

'You talk straight, Lawrence,' he declared.

'If I'm talkin' to a friend,' nodded Larry.

'Do what you have to do tomorrow, and don't be worryin' about me,' offered Moses. 'I'll mind what you said — and I thank you for sayin' it.'

Larry elected to sit watch until midnight, and this was to be his night for playing counsellor and comforter to his oddly-assorted allies. Homer joined him at the edge of the brush before seeking sleep.

'Somethin' I need to get off my chest — else I don't reckon I'll sleep.'

'Get it off your chest then,' invited Larry. 'I want all of us rested, clear-headed and keen-eyed when we move again. So you sure need your sleep.'

'I never got around to makin' my will,' confided Homer. 'But, if tomorrow's my last day on earth, that won't stop Theodora and the old sow and mealy-mouthed Orville from takin' over the store. I don't care about that, Larry. Not if I'm gonna be too dead to care . . . '

'I got a hunch you'll live through this ruckus,' shrugged Larry. 'But keep talkin'.'

'What I do care about is my share of the bounty of Carrizo,' Homer grimly declared. 'You said equal shares . . . '

'Seems fair.'

'Couldn't be fairer. But you got to promise me somethin'. If I'm killed and you survive, promise me Theodora won't get her greedy paws on my share. Damn it, Larry, I'd be the most restless stiff in the graveyard. Do what you like with my share. Keep it for yourself if you want. Just make sure Theodora don't see a dime of it.'

'You got my word,' sighed Larry. 'Now will you, for the love of Mike, go get your sleep?'

'It wouldn't be decent, her gettin' it,' grouched Homer, as he rose to leave. 'She's gonna divorce me anyway. Not that I'm complainin' about *that*.'

Less than 15 minutes later, Larry shrugged irritably. Three visitors this time. They moved around to squat in front of him, partially obscuring his view of the ridge. Mapache was their spokesman, but by no means the only speaker; as usual Pepi and Bobo threw in their ten cents worth.

'We have talked, Senor Lawrence,

and we are agreed,' began Mapache.

'And now you want to help yourselves to some caballos and get the hell out of here,' guessed Larry. 'Try it, and, when you finally get around to smilin' again, you won't show so many teeth.'

'You do us injustice, senor,' protested Mapache.

'We will fight bandidos,' asserted Bobo.

'Because,' explained Pepi, 'we are poor hombres who wish to be rich hombres.'

'But, to collect our share of the dinero, we must go back to Rodriguez?' asked Mapache.

'No way we can dodge that,' nodded Larry. 'Too bad, caballeros, but it can't be helped. You'll be back in the county jail a couple minutes after the sheriff sights you. The trouble is, fellers, you can't try a stagecoach hold-up without breakin' the law.'

'Ah, si,' sighed Bobo.

'But the gringo sheriff will think kindly of us, no?' suggested Mapache.

'For we are brave hombres who fought El Capitan.'

'Tell you what I'll do,' offered Larry. 'I'll make sure your dinero's stashed snug in some Rodriguez bank. It'll be waitin' for you after the law's through with you. And I'll put in a good word for you with the sheriff, ask him to plead for leniency when the circuit-judge holds court.'

'To help to fight El Capitan,' opined Pepi. 'This pardons us for tryin' to rob the coach, no?'

'I wouldn't reckon so,' grinned Larry. 'But maybe the judge'll go easy on you.'

'We sleep now?' asked Bobo, yawning.

'Sleep now,' nodded Mapache.

To Larry's great relief, no others came to seek his advice or reassurance, nor to extract promises from him. Stretch spelled him at midnight. Moses took over from Stretch around 3.15 a.m. and was still watching the ridge, wary-eyed and cold-nerved when, at sun-up, the hunters rose from their blankets.

'Cold tack again,' said Larry, dropping to one knee beside him. He was about to use his field-glasses. 'Go eat your share while I snoop on them heroes.'

A half-hour later, he rejoined his companions and issued orders. Stretch's pinto was saddled already.

'I don't have to spell it out for you,' Larry told him. 'We can't budge till we're sure they've all moved on. But take your time, amigo. Ride a half-circle over thataway . . . ' He gestured, 'make for the hogsback from the west end. And, if it's clear, signal me — but from the near slope.'

'Looks like it'll be a right fine day,' Stretch remarked, as he mounted. 'Right fine day for a showdown.'

The wagon was readied, the other animals saddled, all gear packed. They followed Larry to the south side of the brush, there to await their next glimpse of the taller Texan. Some 45 minutes later, Stretch reappeared, descending the near slope of the ridge, waving his Stetson.

'That's it,' said Larry. 'We move on now.'

With the Daggetts on the wagon seat, Homer in back and the other men mounted, the calico tied to the tailgate, they broke from the brush and followed track of their quarry to where Stretch awaited them.

'Not too steep this side,' he called to Moses. 'Other side's about the same. So drivin' 'em up and over'll be easy enough.' To his partner he remarked, 'Spine of the ridge is clear. I saw their dust south.'

'All open land beyond the ridge?' asked Larry.

'Nope.' Stretch grinned encouragingly. 'Plenty cover. Rock-mounds, brush, plenty timber.'

'Bueno,' nodded Larry. 'Let's go.'

Moses whipped up the team and put them to the slope, the Texans and the Mexicans moving up to either side. In back, Homer braced a foot against the tailgate and firmly gripped two legs of the tripod supporting the Gatling. He was equally careful when, after crossing the spine of the ridge, the wagon made the southern descent. Without mishap, wagon and riders cleared the ridge and pressed on to the south, track of their quarry fresher now.

It was 10.45 a.m. when Larry called a halt at the south side of a dried-out arroyo. The 8-feet high signpost positioned there proved they had reached the border.

'Two miles south, the spy said,' he reminded the Mexicans, as he swung down. 'Time to rig ourselves like Carrizo's own men.'

Verna wasn't required to withdraw into the wagon bed. While Stretch tied his and Larry's animals behind the rig and set the calico free, his partner and the three jumpy thieves hurried to a straggle of brush, toting their disguises. When they emerged a short time later, less than comfortable in attire stripped from dead and wounded desperadoes, Verna boosted the trio's spirits with an admiring remark. Stretch grinned at Larry and observed, 'You are one mean-lookin' Mex, and that's the pure truth.'

Larry settled the floppy-brimmed sombrero more securely on his head, scowled impatiently and gave the order to move on. As he swung astride the white horse, he traded glances with his partner, sharing the wagon bed with Homer now and hefting a Winchester.

'It seemed like a good idea when I first dreamed it up,' he growled. 'Well — it could still work.'

'It better,' retorted Stretch.

'Remember, Homer,' called Larry. 'At our first sight of Carrizo guards, that's when you trade places with Moses and Verna.'

'I'll be ready,' promised the gunsmith.

'Gatling loaded and ready?' demanded Larry.

'Loaded and ready,' nodded Homer. 'And every other ammunition-belt in close reach.'

'So here we go again, huh runt?'

challenged Stretch.

'Ain't that the truth,' agreed Larry. 'C'mon — move!'

Onward they pressed, Larry and the thieves leading while, two miles to the south, the returning raiders were welcomed noisily by the half-dozen rifle-packing guards patroling the north rim of the wide basin that had been El Capitan's stronghold for almost a year.

On the floor of the basin, the hacienda abandoned by a wealthy rancher was centrally located, commanding pride of place among the other buildings of the Rancho del Rosa, the bunkhouses and adobes that had accommodated a hundred or more vaqueros and servants. As Carrizo's demands had been made at gunpoint, Don Pasquale de Tovar had departed without protest while secretly praying the reign of terror would be of short duration. And now the many corrals of Rancho del Rosa, some 200 feet south of the main building, accommodated the horses of Carrizo's army of cutthroats, homicidal gunmen and anti-social misfits, rogues who hailed him as their superior in intelligence and a brilliant strategist. If they did not regard him as presidential material, they kept this opinion to themselves and stayed healthy.

Over-indulgence had thickened the physique of the ambitious Ricardo Carrizo. Portly in the military garb to which he was addicted, a sky-blue tunic with gold braid and brass buttons, dark-blue, yellow-striped britches tucked into highly-polished, knee-high riding boots, he squatted like a dandified budha behind the big desk in what had been Don Pasquale's study and was now the office of El Capitan, with comfortable living quarters adjoining. The mustache was a thin, lovingly-tended line above the petulant, thick-lipped mouth, the eyes a mite bulgy and the nose snub. Ugly he was, but, like megalomaniacs the world over, convinced he presented an imposing, awe-inspiring demeanor.

From where he lounged by the open window, Carrizo's chief henchman, the bulky and lethal Hernando Torres reported the return of the Rodriguez raiding party.

'Casualties, but not too many.'

'Do you see Ignacio?' demanded Carrizo.

'He comes now,' smiled Torres. 'He carries a sack, Capitan. A very large sack.'

'American dollars for the cause!' chuckled Carizo. He rose and strutted to the great iron safe in the rear corner and unlocked it with the key that never left his person. Opening the door wide, he invited Torres to admire the contents, almost every shelf containing bundles of banknotes. 'You see, Hernando? Soon there will be more — much more. And then we will march on Mexico City. The army will be mine, Melgosa will flee in fear for his life and I, Don Ricardo, will appoint myself president!'

'I congratulate you in advance, Capitan,' grinned Torres.

The triumphant Ignacio Lopez, leader of the Rodriguez raid, made his entrance with his back bowed under the weight of his burden and was accorded a hero's welcome. Onto the desk they emptied the sack, Carrizo's eyes dilating in glee. They toasted one another in tequila, lit cigarillos and set about tallying the loot and packing it into the safe.

'But what of Fernando's scouting party?' Torres demanded of Lopez. 'You did not encounter them while returning to headquarters?'

'They are still at Castejon, I suppose,' shrugged Lopez. 'These expeditions take time, Hernando.' He leered and winked. 'And maybe Fernando found a whore-house.'

'Fernando will obey my orders,' mumbled Carrizo. 'He should return today. No later.'

The stolen funds of the Rodriguez banks were tallied and locked in the safe by the time the hunting party noted the rising smoke of Rancho del Rosa on the southern horizon. Larry at once ordered a halt and called for his field-glasses. Stretch fetched them and lounged beside the white horse while Larry focussed on the distant north rim of the basin. They were still a long way from their goal, but he saw what he expected to see, the moving figures, barely visible riflemen patroling the rim.

'All right — not much farther,' he announced. 'You all know what you have to do. So everybody get set. Stay loose, stay cool, keep your eyes peeled and your hardware ready.'

At about this time, traveling a half-mile ahead of A Company, Sergeant Thomas Corrigan reined up beside the border-marker and surveyed it resentfully. He hated what he saw and what he read, the brief inscription on the plank nailed to the post. It didn't say much but, in his opinion, too much. Undoubtedly, he was sitting his mount on the Mexican border.

'Well, the hell with it,' he scowled. 'If them rebs could travel right on by, why shouldn't the U.S. cavalry? Well — A Company anyway.'

He surrendered to his first rebellious impulse, dismounted and, after much sweating and tugging and heaving, managed to haul the post from the ground. He tossed it aside, intending to spell himself before toting it away, finding a safe hiding place for it. And then his misgivings began.

'Nifty Nathan and his damn-blasted map. He'll guess for sure there ought to be a marker here.'

Glowering at the inscribed plank, he toyed with another impulse. The sign was not painted. The inscription had been burned into the wood. With a poker, a special branding iron? Maybe the heated point of a knife-blade.

'Have to get it done fast — but real careful,' he warned himself.

His luck was holding; plenty of wood scattered hereabouts. On the east side of a rock-cluster, he got his fire going, then dragged the signpost over beside it. The knife he had owned many years had a 7-inch blade and was carried under his tunic in a sheath attached to his pants-belt. He held it in the fire, gingerly avoiding burns to his hand. When the point glowed red, he carefully burned the figure '4' into the space below the original inscription. He added the letters 'm' 'i' and 'l' before re-inserting his blade into the fire. This would be a slow chore and — oh, hell! How much time did he have?

'Stay patient or you'll make a hash of it,' he muttered.

Later, his handiwork finished, he made haste to smother the fire under handfuls of earth. His knife wasn't cool enough for re-sheathing. He buried it also, then axiously inspected the added line. It looked good, he decided, Pretty much as though it were part of the original inscription. Well, pretty much would have to do.

'Couldn't take a chance on makin' it fourteen miles,' he mused, 'or twenty-four. Hell, no. Not with Nathan liable to holler for Kepler to fetch his doggone map.'

The signpost was toted back to its hole, repositioned and made fast by his nudging more earth into the hole. It was holding firm when he remounted and headed north to report as ordered.

A Company was moving south at a steady speed when he was sighted by the lead rider, his captain, who promptly raised a hand, signaling a halt.

'Well, Sergeant Corrigan?' Burke challenged as he reined up. 'By now, you *must* have sighted the border marker.'

'We ain't there yet, Captain,' said Corrigan. 'I found a marker, . . . '

'But what?'

'It reads Border of Mexico — four miles south.'

'Could that be correct?' Burke shook his head in exasperation. 'Oh, well, one must presume our maps aren't accurate to the last mile. Have to allow some leeway I suppose. No need for you to leave us again, Sergeant. Stay with us until we reach the marker you found.' He raised his hand again. 'For-waarrrd — ho . . . !'

Eight enemies of the Carrizo band, meanwhile, were unhurriedly advancing on the near rim of the basin, winning the attention of the guards. Mapache waved excitedly and, at Larry's command, began yelling.

'Hey, compadres, look what we bring! We got hostages — gringo hostages — Americano liquor in the wagon . . . !'

The guards traded grins, all but one who remarked, 'Fernando was not ordered to steal a wagon or take hostages. Maybe the patron will approve, but I don't think so.'

The wagon and riders advanced another 20 yards, another 10, before a guard cursed luridly and gasped a warning.

'On the white horse! That is not Gonzalez!'

'I see the dun horse of Fernando Montoya!' cried another, raising his rifle. 'But that rider is not Montoya!'

'They got smart at last!' growled Larry, filling his right hand with Colt. 'Keep that rig rollin', Homer! Stringbean, get your rifle workin'!'

With the apprehensive but obedient thieves fanned out to left and right of him, he spurred the calico forward with his Colt booming. A rifle barked from the rim, but only once. His second bullet accounted for that guard and, rising from behind Homer, Stretch now cut loose with his Winchester. Mapache, Pepi and Bobo were blazing away with their pistols, only one of them scoring; by accident, a slug triggered by Bobo creased a shoulder and caused a guard to howl in agony, drop his rifle and disappear below the rim. That guard descended to where his horse was tethered, struggled astride and continued his descent at speed, yelling the alarm.

Bullets whined about the advancing wagon and riders. One tore through the vehicle, speeding between Stretch and Homer, over the bowed heads of the Daggetts, missing the Gatling and the horses tied behind by mere inches. Pepi loosed a wail and pitched to the dust. Mapache lost his pistol and, with his right arm hanging bloody and useless, grasped for his saddle-horn with his left hand. Two more fast-triggered slugs from Stretch's Winchester, another burst from Larry's Colt, and the nearest guards were down, wounded or dead.

'Now make for the rim and turn the wagon!' bellowed Larry.

He drew the Colt once used by a bandit named Gonzalez, rode to the rim and swung down to survey the scene below. It was an impressive hideout at that. Obviously, Carrizo believed in doing it in style. A rider, the wounded guard, was dropping from his mount in front of the hacienda and hurrying inside. The whole basin floor was coming alive, armed bandidos bounding out of the other buildings, some dashing to the corrals. He glanced over his shoulder. The rear of the wagon was now less than 3 feet from the edge. Stretch had thought to release the saddle-horses before Homer began wheeling the wagon team. The gunsmith now descended, hefting a rifle. Moses and his daughter followed, hurrying to join Larry. He gruffly ordered them to take cover behind the boulders along the edge.

'And keep your eyes on the guards south and both sides — 'case they try rushin' you. Hey, Bobo! Help Mapache off of that horse and take him and Pepi to cover — muy pronto!'

'We hold our fire now, huh?' called Homer.

'No use wastin' bullets,' nodded Larry. 'When you have to use them guns again, you won't be waitin' for an order from me.'

From inside the wagon, Stretch called to him.

'We're as ready as we'll ever be. And that goes double for the Gatling.'

'Yeah, okay.' Larry retreated to the tailgate and began hauling himself over. 'I'll give 'em just one chance to surrender — then the next move's up to Carrizo.' Having boarded the rig, he bellowed at the full strength of his lungs. English with a Texas accent might be lost on a majority of the bandidos, so he voiced his demand in Spanish. 'We are here for Ricardo Carrizo! I demand the surrender of Ricardo Carrizo and all his men! Throw down your arms!' Having delivered that speech, he called to his companions. 'Stay patient. This might take a little time.'

The wounded guard had mumbled his report to an incredulous Carrizo. Equally incredulous, Torres demanded to be told,

'How many of these fools?'

'I see only four riders,' groaned the

wounded man. 'And the one who drives the wagon. But there are more *inside* the wagon!'

'How many men can one wagon carry?' jeered Carrizo. 'They are lunatics, these Americans who dare to . . . ' He tensed, his gaze switching to the door. 'Who . . . ?'

A bug-eyed gunman came hustling in to relay the demand bellowed by Larry. Carrizo promptly burst into laughter and sank into his chair.

'They *must* be lunatics,' Torres said contemptuously.

'How many could hide in one wagon?' leered Carrizo. 'As many as I could order into battle against them? Enough of this crazy comedy, Hernando. You will order forty men to ride to the rim and dispose of these fools. They are to be shown no quarter, understand?'

With his pulse quickening, Homer Gledhill watched the men saddling up far below.

'You're gonna have to use the ace up

your sleeve,' he called to Larry. 'I see better than three dozen of 'em saddlin' up — and I just don't believe they'll ride for the south slope.'

'I see 'em too,' Larry replied. 'They'll rush us, Homer.'

'And they'll sure as hell wish they hadn't of,' growled Stretch.

Away from the corrals surged the heavily-armed riders. Across the basin floor they charged to put their animals to the near slope. Already, some were rising in their stirrups, discharging rifles, and the din of gunfire carried far on the early afternoon air, carried north by a stiff wind.

Moments before, A Company had paused in column by the border marker. Burke was studying it intently and Corrigan thinking, 'Hell's bells, it's just five words and a figure four. How long does he need for readin' it?'

'According to this sign,' frowned the captain, 'we are now four miles north of the Mexican border. I was certain this would be the actual border marker. However . . . '

'What I hear from the south couldn't be more'n a couple miles away,' Corrigan said impatiently. 'You hear it?'

'Gunfire, Captain!' offered the keen eared Corporal Kepler.

'Thank you, Corporal,' nodded Burke. 'I know gunfire when I hear it.'

'Can't you guess what this means?' challenged Corrigan.

'It would seem your prediction has been proved accurate,' conceded Burke. 'The Texans and their companions have stumbled upon a Carrizo encampment — perhaps not the secret headquarters of the band — nevertheless . . . '

'We gonna sit our saddles and jaw about it?' scowled Corrigan. 'Beggin' the captain's pardon, but the army can't leave this chore to a handful of civilians, can it? So what're we waitin' for?'

'Later, we'll discuss your too-informal attitude toward an officer,' Burke said reproachfully. 'Later, Sergeant. After we've investigated the source of this shooting affray.'

He gave the command and, at the double, A Company got moving again.

# 8

## Devil-Gun Justice

Crouched behind the Gatling, Larry watched the fast-shooting horsemen surging up the near slope of the basin. He kept his eyes on them while asking Stretch, 'Any more of our bunch hit?'

'Not yet,' said the taller Texan. 'They're huggin' their cover and doin' fine.'

Sprawled behind boulders along the rim, Homer, Moses and Verna were opening fire on the opposition, the men cutting loose with rifles, the girl doing her utmost with her pistol held in both hands. And they were scoring. The lead rider was knocked from his horse by Homer. Moses put another out of the fight, aiming for a chest and breaking a shoulder. While reloading, Verna rolled over to stare expectantly to the wagon.

And then, hard-eyed and relentless, Larry started the Gatling working.

'Remember the Alamo,' he said grimly.

His first turn of the firing handle emptied two saddles. Three more turns and startled bandidos were wheeling their animals in frantic haste. The chug-chug of the Gatling rose loud and ominous above the pounding of hooves and cries of mortal agony as more riders pitched to the slope.

'Now we raise the sight a mite,' growled Larry, 'and spread trouble down below.'

The next prolonged burst from the Gatling hurtled above the retreating riders and threw the whole Carrizo stronghold into confusion. The effect of those .65 calibre rounds raking the basin floor was spectacular and demoralizing, the heavy missiles plowing through adobe walls, churning up dust and grit in the area between the bunkhouses and the hacienda. One round sped through the window of the room occupied by Carrizo and three of his minions, missed Torres with only inches to spare, struck a corner of the iron safe and ricocheted upward to bore a sizeable hole in the ceiling. Carrizo cursed obscenely and threw himself flat. He yelled to his compadres to follow his example and might as well have saved his breath; they were prone already.

The empty belt was tossed aside and hastily replaced, the attack resumed with a vengeance. In their frantic quest for cover, yelling desperadoes were scurrying in all directions; panic was setting in.

Guards manning the east, west and south areas of the basin-rim had begun working their way around to where the invaders were positioned, but began a disorderly descent when the Gatling's lethal voice was heard. To the basin floor, Larry triggered another merciless hail. Then, as Stretch helped him reload, he warned, 'We better be ready for runaways. If anybody breaks and runs for it, you can bet your double-cinched saddle they'll try for the far side.'

Two rounds had penetrated the wall, putting the fear of hell into the boss-bandido. Carrizo was sweating profusely when he barked orders to Torres.

'Crawl out. Have a vehicle made ready. If we have to run from this place, we will not leave the cash to these gringos! The safe must be placed in a wagon. We will then retreat to the south.'

'To stay would be foolish,' mumbled Torres, as he began crawling to the doorway. 'I have heard of these guns-that-fire-so-fast! We have no chance against . . . !'

'A wagon, Hernando!' wailed Carrizo. 'Hurry!'

From behind boulders on the basin floor, riflemen were concentrating heavy fire on Homer and the Daggetts and all they could see of the wagon. Larry sighted a moving vehicle down there and was about to resume firing when Verna's urgent voice was raised.

'Pa's all bloody!'

Stretch made to descend from the wagon, but was warned back by Homer.

'You stay with Larry and the Gatling! I'll take care of Moses!'

A rifle-slug whined past the gunsmith's left ear as he began moving. His scalp crawled. Hastily he dropped flat to crawl to where the farmer lay. Daggett was conscious and groaning, blood welling from his right side; once too often he had risen above his cover, the better to draw a bead.

'No bullet in me,' he panted, as Homer flopped beside him. 'But — by damn — it sure tore a hunk out of me . . . !'

'Hold this against the wound,' Homer ordered the girl, fishing out a bandana. 'And don't be frettin', Verna. Won't be long before we're patchin' your pa real good.' He retreated to the rear of the wagon for a brief parley with the

Texans. 'You sure scattered 'em, Larry, but this battle ain't won yet. All three of our Mex buddies are out of the fight, wounded and hurtin'. And now Moses too.'

'The hell of it is I have to move now,' muttered Larry. 'I can see a rig over by the hacienda. Three-four hombres loadin' somethin' aboard.' He snatched for the field-glasses passed him by his partner and raised them to his eyes. 'And that 'somethin' looks like a — yeah! A safe! It could be Carrizo about to make a run for it!'

'With mucho dinero,' opined Stretch. 'Most of it greenbacks from banks north of the border.'

'When you move, they'll rush us again,' predicted Homer. 'Nothin' surer.'

'What d'you say, runt?' prodded Stretch. 'You need me along?'

'They need you more,' said Larry, glancing to the Daggetts. 'So take our Winchesters, grab every other gun you can find and make-believe you're a whole platoon.'

'Be right with you, Homer,' Stretch said cheerfully. 'Get on back to your rock.'

Moments later, urged on by Larry, he was dropping from the Conestoga with a rifle under either arm and a box of cartridges stuffed in a pocket. By then, the vehicle ordered by Carrizo was being driven away from the hacienda, southward toward the far slope of the basin, and Larry was hustling through the wagon to climb onto the seat and gather the reins.

He kicked off the brake, yelled to the team and wheeled them to the left to begin circling the basin. Where the ground was potholed or rocky, he guided the hard-running team clear. Twice the vehicle rolled on only two wheels. Once the left front team-leader almost lost its footing at the very edge of the rim, and still he kept them moving at speed.

From the rock where he crouched, Stretch surveyed the scene below and called casually to Homer.

'Seems like you guessed right. Some of 'em gettin' mounted again.'

'They'll rush us!' gasped Homer.

'So?' Stretch grinned and readied a Winchester. 'Let's make 'em regret it.'

Daggett had lost consciousness. His daughter studied his pallid face a few moments, then thumbed back the hammer on her Colt and resumed her firing position, her young eyes fixed on the fanned-out twenty horsemen now putting their animals to the near slope.

'Don't cut loose till I say the word,' drawled Stretch. 'We're gonna have to make every shot count. No wild triggerin', hear?'

Half-way up the slope, the bandidos began raking the rim with rifle-slugs. Stretch, Homer and the girl leveled their weapons and waited — until Stretch growled, 'Now!'

The gunsmith had never heard a Winchester operating at such speed. From a half-kneeling position, Stretch fired, worked the lever-action and fired again, scoring every time. Encouraged, Homer opened up again, emptying a saddle with his first shot. Verna clenched her teeth. The Colt began booming, and now she too was scoring.

Larry, meanwhile, was keeping the wagon-team to a hectic pace and darting glances to the basin-floor, glimpsing the other vehicle at irregular intervals.

'Three spans,' he noted. 'They got six husky teamers haulin' that rig. Well — it looked sizeable, that safe. Likely plenty hefty — and full.'

Nearing the south rim, he won a side-on view of the vehicle now being hauled up the slope by the six broad-backed teamers. The driver, Torres, was just another overweight bandido. But the pudgy individual sharing the seat with the driver, so colorful in his makeshift uniform . . .

'Could that be Carrizo himself? Well, why not? Ain't that just like a boss-bandido cravin' to take over the whole Mex government — that fancy outfit,

237

the gold braid and all? Yeah. That could be Carrizo.'

When he wheeled his team to the right and hauled back on the reins, the Conestoga's tailgate was less than two feet from the rim. He had cut it fine, he reflected, as he applied the brake and clambered over the seat. But that other rig was a clear target from this position. And still some 30 yards from the flat land to the south.

He readied the Gatling and, before peering through the sight, threw a glance to the north side. Eight riders were in retreat again, followed by almost twice as many riderless horses.

Training the Gatling on a point about 10 yards ahead of the other vehicle's team-leaders, he gave the firing handle a half-turn. Dust and shattered rock arose to startle the animals. They began balking. Torres pulled rein frantically and turned to stare at the little he could see of the Conestoga. In Spanish, Larry yelled his challenge.

'That's as far as you go! Leave that

vehicle — with your hands raised!'

Carrizo's retaliation took him by surprise, but only for a moment. At their leader's muttered command, seven men inside the wagon thrust rifles over the sideplanks, lined them on the Conestoga and cut loose with a burst of fire. With rifle-slugs kicking chunks from the tailgate and tearing through the canvas above and to either side of him, Larry growled 'The hell with it,' and turned the firing handle and the Gatling wreaked havoc.

He concentrated his fire on the vehicle, feeling compassion for the terrified team, but none for the minions of the would-be despot. The wagon shuddered from the impact of the .65 calibre rounds. The near rear wheel was suddenly minus three spokes and the canopy shredded. Torres was brandishing a pistol when he pitched from the seat, never to move again. Another man yelled in fear and agony. It was Carrizo, dropping from the seat. On hands and knees he crawled until his strength gave out. Two unscathed bandidos clambered from the rear of the vehicle with their hands raised. In shock, they gaped at the pudgy, brightly-uniformed body of their leader rolling past, rolling 20 yards to come up hard against a boulder.

'Damn and blast!' From his sprawled position at the north rim, left hand clamped to his bullet-gashed right arm, Homer stared fearfully at the taller Texan. 'You hear what I hear? More riders comin' up on us — from behind! Some of 'em must've gotten out — and now we're finished!'

Stretch glanced over his shoulder and Homer took heart from his changing expression, first an incredulous frown, then a wry grin.

'I wouldn't be frettin', Homer,' he drawled. 'They don't look like no Mexican soldier-boys.'

'Troopers!' cried Verna. 'Come to rescue us! Oh, don't they look just beautiful?'

'Right purty,' agreed Stretch. 'A mite

late. But right purty.'

The gunsmith loosed a sigh of relief and turned, the better to view the impressive arrival of A Company, 2nd. U.S. Cavalry. Onward they came, the captain and the two noncoms leading the column of troopers.

'Hey, Captain . . . !' Corrigan called. 'Looks like the fightin's started already! You gonna let a handful of civilians steal our thunder?'

'Damn it, no!' scowled Burke. He reined up for a few words, his questing eyes switching from the huddled and groaning Mexicans to the Daggetts, then to Stretch. 'Quickly now,' he urged. 'What's the situation here? You've engaged El Capitan's forces?'

'You could put it that way, Colonel,' nodded Stretch.

'You heard the sergeant call me 'Captain',' chided Burke.

'Well, a full colonel is what you ought to be,' Stretch said admiringly. 'Yessir, Cap'n, that's the Carrizo gang down there. My partner circled round to cut off their retreat and . . . '

'I've heard enough,' said Burke, unsheathing his sabre. 'Sergeant Corrigan relay my order to the standard-bearer and the bugler. Sound the charge!'

Elatedly, Corrigan relayed the order and, to Verna's glee, A Company advanced to the rim and began a fast descent to the basin floor, the noncoms brandishing pistols, troopers readying carbines. They made a stirring, pulse-quickening sight in the harsh sunlight, pounding down the slope, and the few survivors of the Carrizo band were even more impressed than young and excitable Verna. The Gatling had demoralized the once bloodthirsty, trigger-happy bandidos; the sudden appearance of the cavalry was the finishing touch, albeit somewhat of an anti-climax.

Larry, seeing the survivors of his last attack moving down to the basin-floor with their hands raised, threw a puzzled glance northward, saw the charging troopers and wondered, 'Where the hell'd *they* come from?'

It then occurred to him that Stretch, Homer or Verna might bungle the explanations to which the army was entitled — especially Stretch. Time for him to rejoin his companions, ready, willing and able to counter the questions and probable accusations of the officer in charge. He secured the Gatling, clambered through to the seat, gathered the reins and kicked off the brake. The Conestoga moved again, back to the north side of the basin-rim.

Down below, troopers were rounding up wounded and unscathed survivors. Not a shot had been fired by soldiers or bandidos, much to the chagrin of Sergeant Corrigan and the confusion of Captain Burke.

'Burial detail, Corporal Kepler,' he ordered. 'Secure all prisoners, render whatever first aid is possible for the wounded. Then a burial detail. Usual procedure. All casualties to be searched for identification.'

'Our damn cavalry luck,' grouched

Corrigan. 'If we'd gotten here a mite earlier . . . '

'It would seem these civilians — two of whom you so admire — used a stolen Gatling to good advantage,' Burke said coldly. 'And now, by thunder, they'd better be ready to explain their actions. You will accompany me, Sergeant.'

As they climbed to the north rim, Corrigan remarked, 'I don't reckon their actions need much explainin'. Plain enough what they did. The gunsmith repaired the Gatling and they fetched it along, tagged track of the Rodriguez raidin' party all the way to here, and licked the whole damn Carrizo outfit.'

'That Gatling is army ordnance,' Burke reminded him. 'Stolen army property.'

'This it is,' shrugged Corrigan.

Reaching the north rim, they dismounted. Burke, a stickler for protocol, identified himself and the sergeant. Stretch sketched him a casual salute and reciprocated by introducing the victorious civilians.

'Emerson's my handle. You can call me Stretch. That's my partner, Larry Valentine, patchin' Mister Moses Daggett. This here's Mister Homer Gledhill, and that purty little lady is Moses' daughter Verna — her that's comfortin' them three shot-up caballeros best way she knows how.'

'Quit your whinin'!' Larry called gruffly to the groaning trio. 'I'll start workin' on you when I'm through doctorin' Moses. Hey, stringbean, fetch more whiskey.'

'Comin',' grunted Stretch. 'Uh, I plumb forgot to introduce our Mex buddies. They're called Mapache, Pepi and Bobo.'

'Now see here, Mister Valentine . . .' began Burke.

'All right, all right, you got questions,' muttered Larry, not deigning to glance his way. 'Just don't make me no speech, Captain — what's your given name anyway?'

'Nathan,' frowned Burke.

'All right, Nate, I'll be glad to tell you everything you need to know,' said Larry. 'Why waste time shootin' questions? Better you stay quiet while I explain what we did.'

He took the bottle passed him by Stretch and an item of female underwear purloined from Verna's gear and set about improvising a dressing for Moses' wound, while Burke sternly accused him.

'You are jailbreakers — fugitives from justice.'

'Keep your shirt on, Nate,' growled Larry. 'Hey, Verna, I'm through patchin' your pa. You see what you can do for Homer while I tend Mapache and his buddies. This way, Nate . . .'

Burke and the sergeant had no option but to follow Larry to the pain-wracked Mexicans. Corrigan peeled off his tunic — the heat was intense — produced a bandana and began giving what aid he could.

'Sure, I busted us out of the Rodriguez calaboose,' Larry continued.

'What the hell else could I do? Them damn bandidos might've set fire to the place, and that lard-bellied deputy was spooked and useless.'

'So you took the initiative,' nodded Burke. 'But you are still fugitives.'

'Not for long,' Larry assured him. 'We'll all be headed back to Rodriguez.'

'And get throwed in jail again?' frowned Corrigan.

'Listen, there's a bank cashier headed for Rodriguez, ought to arrive any time,' said Larry. 'He works for a Lawson City bank that got robbed and he can identify the robbers. So we should fret, Stretch and me? One look and he'll clear us.'

Rough surgery on the doleful trio was finally completed. Burke then began a reprimand, only to be interrupted by a thoughtful Larry.

'Might be better if we drop the Daggetts off at Castejon. Bound to be a doctor there, and Moses needs a real professional patchin' job — better than I cound manage. Uh huh. Then we'll head for Rodriguez.'

'The Gatling gun is stolen property of . . . ' began Burke.

'Sure,' nodded Larry. 'But Homer's a gunsmith. We were countin' on him to get it workin' again. You sayin' we should've left it in the jailyard — for Carrizo's raiders to find and steal? How d'you like the idea of El Capitan ownin' a U.S. Army Gatling?'

'So you took the Gatling so them bandidos wouldn't get their dirty paws on it, huh?' grinned Corrigan. 'Well, the Second Cavalry is sure beholden.'

'Sergeant . . . !' gasped Burke.

'You're entirely welcome — only too glad to oblige,' shrugged Larry. 'And, now that we're though with it, it's okay by me if you take it back to Mesa Valdez.'

'You're too kind,' sneered Burke.

'Think nothin' of it,' said Larry. 'This Conestoga wagon though, we'll have to use it some more. Need it for givin' Mapache and his buddies a gentle run back to Rodriguez. And there's somethin' else we'll need it for.' He jerked a thumb. 'You'll find a safe, a big safe, in Carrizo's getaway rig. My hunch is it's full of the dinero, the loot from all those bank raids. There'll be a reward, and I promised my friends equal shares, you know? So I'm deliverin' that safe to a Rodriguez bank.'

'And then them bankers can talk turkey, wire all the other banks,' guessed Stretch. 'Work out which bank lost how much dinero — and stuff like that.'

'You can't just . . . ' Burke gesticulated agitatedly, 'haul that much money in a Conestoga from here to Castejon and then on to Rodriguez! Such a massive quantity of cash warrants a suitable escort . . . !'

'I want to thank you for that mighty generous offer, Nate,' Larry said warmly. 'Easy to savvy how you made captain so young.' He nodded to Corrigan. 'Sarge, you got a good officer here.'

'Well, he's shapin' up pretty good,' conceded Corrigan.

'A dozen troopers ought to do it,' decided Larry. 'With the Sarge here, huh? On account of he acts damn near as smart-brained as you, Nate.'

'I have never — in my entire military career . . . ' breathed Burke, 'encountered such — such bare-faced impertinence — such unmitigated nerve . . . '

'Speakin' of nerve,' remarked Stretch. 'It must've took plenty of that for you to lead a whole company of U.S. cavalry over the border into Mexico.'

'I would *never* do *that!*' retorted Burke. 'I estimate, Mister Emerson, we are still a full two miles from Mexico!'

'That's how I calculate it,' offered Corrigan.

'Funny,' frowned Stretch. 'I recall we passed the border-marker . . . '

'Uh huh,' nodded Larry. 'Signpost couple miles back.'

'Well, you maybe don't read so

good,' Corrigan said quickly. 'It reads Border Of Mexico Four Miles South.'

'Exactly,' said Burke.

For a fleeting moment, Larry matched glances with the sergeant. Corrigan's expression was eloquent; he was begging.

'Well . . . ' Larry shrugged casually. 'What's a few miles either way?'

'We settled Carrizo's hash,' said Stretch. 'That's what's important.'

'How about your prisoners, Nate?' demanded Larry. 'They're all Mexican, so who d'you turn 'em over to?'

'My obvious course is to take them to northwest to Rodneyville,' said Burke. 'The sheriff of Rodney County is a personal friend. I believe there are rurales stationed at Llano Seco, which is only a few miles from Rodneyville on the Mexican side. We'll telegraph them from Rodneyville and the sheriff will hold the captives until an escort party arrives.' He added pointedly, 'You may be sure the hand-over will be well and truly in line with correct procedure.'

251

'Sure enough,' grinned Larry. 'You'll do it right.'

* * *

It was not until mid-morning of the following day that Larry committed Tom Corrigan to his cause. The trouble-shooters were riding either side of the sergeant, out of earshot of the wagon and escorting troopers. A trooper drove, Verna keeping him company, Homer sharing the wagon bed with the safe and the other wounded.

Corrigan sweated when, in his blunt way, Larry assured him, 'I already guessed who messed with that border marker.'

'Me too,' grinned Stretch. 'Some proddy three-striper itchin' for a fight. Irish, I bet.'

'Listen, if the captain ever found out . . . ' began Corrigan.

'He won't learn of it from us,' said Larry. 'Only, if we have to keep our mouths shut, it's gonna cost you.'

'Anything,' sighed Corrigan. 'You just name it.'

'In Rodriguez, I'll have to do some lyin',' drawled Larry. 'In a good cause, mind. But lies, Sarge. And you're gonna back me up.'

'Well — uh — I'd better know what kind of lies,' frowned Corrigan. He listed incredulously as Larry calmly confided his intentions. 'Great day in the mornin'! I always heard you were cunning, Valentine, but . . .'

'He can be powerful sneaky, my ol' buddy,' remarked Stretch.

'The whole bounty?' challenged Corrigan. 'Every dollar of it?'

'And I'll make sure every party gets his share,' declared Larry. 'You leery of me, Sarge? Think we'd keep it for ourselves — cheat on them that threw in with us?'

'Hell, no,' shrugged Corrigan.' That's somethin' else I've heard, and I believe it. You never double-cross your friends.'

'Deal?' prodded Larry.

'Deal,' said Corrigan.

Within a half-hour of their arrival in Castejon, Homer, the Daggetts and Mapache and cronies were discreetly installed in a hotel. Castejon's doctor was summoned and Moses was his first patient. To Homer, Larry announced his change of heart.

'Those poor dumb Mexicans — yeah.' Resting comfortably on the bed in his room, the gunsmith grinned approvingly. 'They're hurtin' and they're scared. And, when you get right down to it, they made it all possible, didn't they? If they hadn't stolen the Gatling . . . '

'*You* helped make it all possible,' Larry reminded him. 'If you hadn't set the Gatling to rights . . . '

'So Larry figures you ought to be just as dead as them three thieves,' explained Stretch. 'And I go along with it, Homer. To me, it seems mighty reasonable.'

Homer's eyebrows shot up.

'Are you sayin' . . . ?'

'I'm sayin' she'd damn quick change

254

her mind about a divorce,' grinned Larry, 'if she found out you collected a piece of the reward.'

'That's so,' nodded Homer. 'It'd be just like it always was. I'd never get to enjoy a dime of it.'

'So rest easy,' soothed Larry. 'We'll be seein' you.'

★ ★ ★

The return of the Conestoga to Rodriguez with a cavalry escort caused the predictable stir. They arrived around 2 p.m. of a fine, clear day, the Texans sharing the wagon seat, their horses tied in back, Corrigan riding level and the escorting troopers flanking them.

From the porch of the sheriff's office, Marlowe and his deputies stared hard at them. Deputy Dodson was impassive, but Deputy Hines showing plenty of expression, the hostile kind. Curious locals converged on the scene as Larry stalled the rig in front of the office. He nodded casually to the lawmen.

'Howdy,' he greeted. 'You ever find out who owns this wagon? We turned the Gatling over to the cavalry, but . . . '

'But we needed this rig for haulin' the loot,' explained Stretch. 'Big iron safe from El Capitan's hideaway.'

'We know about that,' said Marlowe. 'Captain Burke was kind enough to wire me the news from Rodneyville.'

'Telegraph workin' again, huh?' prodded Larry.

'Works just fine,' offered Dodson. He summoned up a grin and, with his chief, descended from the porch to converse with the Texans. Hines stayed on the porch and seethed, glaring balefully at Larry. 'We got another wire this mornin' — from Lawson City?'

'No need for Mister Tatlock to come clear you,' offered Marlowe. 'Those tall hold-up artists were apprehended by the Uvalde County authorities day before yesterday. They were taken to Lawson, where Tatlock made a positive identification.'

'So that clears you,' said Dodson. 'And you got an apology comin'.'

'Forget it,' shrugged Larry. 'It's us ought to apologize for bustin' out of your jail.' He matched stares with Marlowe. 'But you can guess how it was for us. We couldn't take a chance on the raiders startin' a fire — or findin' that Gatling.'

'So you took the Gatling to El Capitan's hideout and fought and licked the whole outfit,' frowned Marlowe.

'They sure did, Sheriff,' declared Corrigan.

'But you didn't go it alone, right?' challenged Marlowe. 'What of Homer Gledhill and those Mexicans?'

Larry sighed heavily and turned to the sergeant.

'You tell 'em. I don't have the heart for it.'

'The others . . . ' Corrigan shrugged uncomfortably. 'Well — they weren't as lucky as Valentine and Emerson. Got shot up bad.'

'I'm gonna miss them four,' muttered

257

Stretch. 'When it came to the showdown, they sure did their share.'

'I'll have to break the news to Mrs Gledhill,' said Marlowe, 'while you delivery your cargo to the Occidental Bank. Burl will show you the way. The Occidental will undertake to arrange distribution of the recovered funds. And — uh — you'll claim the reward on Carrizo?'

'We ain't bounty-hunters,' drawled Stretch. 'But we figure we done earned that twenty thousand.'

'Thirty,' corrected Marlowe. 'Territorial government upped the ante.'

'Carrizo was quite a threat while he lasted,' Dodson pointed out. 'Some of our territorial big shots likely feared he'd take over New Mexico and the Arizona Territory as well as his own country.'

At the Occidental Bank, the safe was unloaded and toted into the vault. Unlocking it was no problem, Larry having taken the key from Carrizo's body. Then, while his cashiers set about the heavy chore of tallying the contents, the manager shook the Texans' hands, thanked them warmly and announced his willingness to endorse their claim for the bounty.

Some 5 days later, Larry and Stretch visited Castejon again, this time to present large sums of cash to the men convalescing from their wounds at the Alhambra Hotel. Mapache, Pepi and Bobo promptly insisted they were fully recovered and tried to leave their beds; they had to be restrained by the Texans and the local doctor.

'In five or six days you'll be healthy enough to travel,' the medico assured them. 'Until then, you have to rest. And you can kill time by planning how you'll use all that money.'

Moses Daggett and his daughter were dumbstruck. When he finally found his voice, the Arkansas farmer was almost incoherent.

'All this — just for us?'

'It's too much,' protested Verna.

'You earned it,' insisted Larry.

'That's your share. Think about it a while, and you'll soon decide how much you can do with it.'

'Next Daggett farm'll be somethin' to see,' predicted Stretch.

'Best in Arkansas,' enthused Verna. 'What d'you you say, Pa? We goin' back to Arkansas?'

'Like Lawrence said, we'll think about it a while,' said Moses.

Homer, sitting by the window of his room with his arm in a sling, watched the Texans dump several wads of banknotes onto the bed and said, 'I don't believe it.'

'Give it time, Homer,' grinned Stretch. 'You'll soon get used to bein' rich.'

'Remember what you said in the Rodriguez county jail, first time we talked?' Larry said gently. 'You'd be the happiest man in the world if you could get far from Rodriguez, find a quiet town, change your name and start all over again.'

'And stay woman-shy the rest of your

life,' recalled Stretch.

'Now you can do it,' said Larry. 'In style.'

'Tell me somethin',' frowned Homer. 'How much of that bounty are you keepin' for yourselves. You should have the biggest share.'

'Oh, we got plenty,' shrugged Stretch. 'It's different with us, Homer. Mucho dinero spooks us. From Rodriguez to here, totin' all this bounty money, we sweated for every mile of the way.'

'Just rest yourself and make your plans, Homer,' urged Larry, as they turned to leave. 'We promised to meet Marshal Rodd in a saloon. Got some celebratin' to catch up on.' From the doorway, the tall men grinned encouragingly at the gunsmith. 'Homer, how's it feel to be dead?'

'And rid of Theodora?' asked Stretch.

'I guess you could say . . . ' chuckled Homer, 'she's a woman worth dyin' for.'

# Epilogue

HOMER GLEDHILL did not stay woman-shy the rest of his life. A year after re-settling in Willis, California, under the assumed name EDWARD HILL, he wooed and won a widow, the owner of a restaurant in that town. Predictably, this lady bore no resemblance to Theodora, physically or temperamentally. It was a congenial and, to both parties, very satisfactory marriage.

Surprisingly, MAPACHE, PEPI and BOBO did quite well for themselves after traveling from Castejon and Tampico. Having acquired capital, they decided they could afford to abandon petty thievery and go straight. They went straight to a waterfront cantina overlooking the Gulf of Mexico, took a liking to the place and persuaded the owner to sell. The owner was only too willing, trade having been slack of late. But the luck of the three misfits was riding high. The enterprising Mapache acquired a formidable supply of raw alcohol. Instead of watering the booze at the cantina to cheat the customers, he and his buddies gave it an extra kick and, within the week, had to hire two additional barkeeps to cope with the rush of new business.

MOSES DAGGETT and daughter VERNA re-established themselves on a verdant farm in Calloway, Arkansas. In her 20th year, Verna married the local schoolmaster who, as well as becoming a devoted husband, set about educating his pretty wife and teaching her the airs and graces of a lady of quality. At first bemused, Moses came to admire his daughter's fine manners and new dignity.

THEODORA GLEDHILL remarried two years after the demise of the Carrizo gang. Her new husband, like a lamb to the slaughter, moved in with his bride, her mother and her brother. To his credit, he endured this domestic arrangement for three whole weeks, after which he put his last few dollars on Number 13 at the roulette layout at the Broken Spur Saloon, reasoning there was no way his luck could worsen. The wheel spun and, eventually, the dancing pellet settled snugly in the hollow numbered 13. After rallying from his shock, he collected his winnings, purchased and disposed of a shot of bourbon and, when last seen, was driving a rented buggy out of town at high speed. The livery stable owner never recovered his buggy and Theodora never saw her second husband again.

President JUAN MELGOSA's personal secretary conveyed his profound thanks to the officer commanding the 2nd. U.S. Cavalry for the co-operation of A Company in rounding up the survivors of El Capitan's murderous band. With great tact, the secretary assured the officer commanding that, under the happy circumstances, his government would make no protest to Washington concerning the entry into Mexican territory of American troops.

Incensed, CAPTAIN NATHAN BURKE interrogated Sergeant THOMAS CORRIGAN for almost 45 minutes in the commanding officer's private quarters and, unflinchingly, Corrigan stood his ground and stuck to his story. The captain had read the inscription on the marker, had he not? Mexican Border 4 Miles South. If that marker gave incorrect information regarding the exact location of the border, why blame him?

Thereafter, Burke vigorously campaigned for the inspection and rechecking of all border markers between Mexico and its neighbours to the immediate north, Arizona, New Mexico and Texas, demanding that Mexican and American teams of surveyors be ordered into this most vital operation. For several years Burke pleaded, petitioned and pulled strings, even taking a furlough and journeying to

Washington to seek an audience with the president of the United States. Precise marking of national borders became his obsession and irritated hundreds of officials, including the President himself. Corrigan was human enough to feel secretly ashamed, but never confided the truth to even his most trusted cronies. And, though ashamed, he often aroused the curiosity of his fellow-noncoms by chuckling for no apparent cause, as though remembering an old joke.

LAWRENCE VALENTINE and WOODVILLE 'STRETCH' EMERSON, as was their habit, put all thought of this latest escape behind them after quitting Castejon. Their 'Remember The Alamo' celebration with MARSHAL CASIUS RODD had left them a mite hung-over, but as restless as ever. They resumed their wanderings, still itchy-footed, still a threat to the lawless of the frontier.

Leopards cannot change their spots, nor trouble-shooters their ways.

CALABOOSE EXPRESS
WHISKEY GULCH
THE ALIBI TRAIL
SIX GUILTY MEN
FORT DILLON
IN PURSUIT OF QUINCEY BUDD
HAMMER'S HORDE
TWO GENTLEMEN FROM TEXAS
HARRIGAN'S STAR
TURN THE KEY ON EMERSON
ROUGH ROUTE TO RODD COUNTY
SEVEN KILLERS EAST
DAKOTA DEATH-TRAP
GOLD, GUNS & THE GIRL
RUCKUS AT GILA WELLS
LEGEND OF COYOTE FORD
ONE HELL OF A SHOWDOWN
EMERSON'S HEX
SIX GUN WEDDING
THE GOLD MOVERS
WILD NIGHT IN WIDOW'S PEAK
THE TINHORN MURDER CASE
TERROR FOR SALE
HOSTAGE HUNTERS
WILD WIDOW OF WOLF CREEK
THE LAWMAN WORE BLACK

THE DUDE MUST DIE
WAIT FOR THE JUDGE
HOLD 'EM BACK!
WELLS FARGO DECOYS
WE RIDE FOR CIRCLE 6
THE CANNON MOUND GANG
5 BULLETS FOR JUDGE BLAKE
BEQUEST TO A TEXAN
THEY'LL HANG BILLY FOR SURE
SLOW WOLF AND DAN FOX
THE NO NAME GANG
DOUBLE SHUFFLE
CHALLENGE THE LEGEND
REVENGE IS THE SPUR

## THE CROOKED SHERIFF
### John Dyson

Black Pete Bowen quit Texas with a burning hatred of men who try to take the law into their own hands. But he discovers that things aren't much different in the silver mountains of Arizona.

## THEY'LL HANG BILLY
## FOR SURE:
### Larry & Stretch
### Marshall Grover

Billy Reese, the West's most notorious desperado, was to stand trial. From all compass points came the curious and the greedy, the riff-raff of the frontier. Suddenly, a crazed killer was on the loose — but the Texas Trouble-Shooters were there, girding their loins for action.

# RIDERS OF RIFLE RANGE
## Wade Hamilton

Veterinarian Jeff Jones did not like open warfare — but it was there on Scrub Pine grass. When he diagnosed a sick bull on the Endicott ranch as having the contagious blackleg disease, he got involved in the warfare — whether he liked it or not!

# BEAR PAW
## Nevada Carter

Austin Dailey traded two cows to a pair of Indians for a bay horse, which subsequently disappeared. Tracks led to a secret hideout of fugitive Indians — and cattle thieves. Indians and stockmen co-operated against the rustlers. But it was Pale Woman who acted as interpreter between her people and the rangemen.

## THE WEST WITCH
### Lance Howard

Detective Quinton Hilcrest journeys west, seeking the Black Hood Bandits' lost fortune. Within hours of arriving in Hags Bend, he is fighting for his life, ensnared with a beautiful outcast the town claims is a witch! Can he save the young woman from the angry mob?

## GUNS OF THE PONY EXPRESS
### T. M. Dolan

Rich Zennor joined the Pony Express venture at the start, as second-in-command to tough Denning Hartman. But Zennor had the problems of Hartman believing that they had crossed trails in the past, and the fact that he was strongly attached to Hartman's Indian girl, Conchita.

## BLACK JO OF THE PECOS
**Jeff Blaine**

Nobody knew where Black Josephine Callard came from or whither she returned. Deputy U.S. Marshal Frank Haggard would have to exercise all his cunning and ability to stay alive before he could defeat her highly successful gang and solve the mystery.

## RIDE FOR YOUR LIFE
**Johnny Mack Bride**

They rode west, hoping for a new start. Then they met another broken-down casualty of war, and he had a plan that might deliver them from despair. But the only men who would attempt it would be the truly brave — or the desperate. They were both.

## THE NIGHTHAWK
### Charles Burnham

While John Baxter sat looking at the ruin that arsonists had made of his log house, a stranger rode into the yard. Baxter and Walt Showalter partnered up and re-built the house. But when it was dynamited, they struck back — and all hell broke loose.

## MAVERICK PREACHER
### M. Duggan

Clay Purnell was hopeful that his posting to Capra would be peaceable enough. However, on his very first day in town he rode into trouble. Although loath to use his .45, Clay found he had little choice — and his likeness to a notorious bank robber didn't help either!

## SIXGUN SHOWDOWN
### Art Flynn

After years as a lawman elsewhere, Dan Herrick returned to his old Arizona stamping ground to find that nesters were being driven from their homesteads by ruthless ranchers. Before putting away his gun once and for all, Dan forced a bloody and decisive showdown.

## RIDE LIKE THE DEVIL!
### Sam Gort

Ben Trunch arrived back on the Big T only to find that land-grabbing was in progress. He confronted Luke Fletcher, saloon-keeper and town boss, with what was happening, and was immediately forced to ride for his life. But he got the chance to put it all right in the end.

## SLOW WOLF AND DAN FOX:
### Larry & Stretch
### Marshall Grover

The deck was stacked against an innocent man. Larry Valentine played detective, and his investigation propelled the Texas Trouble-Shooters into a gun-blazing fight to the finish.

## BRANAGAN'S LAW
### Alan Irwin

To Angus Flint, the valley was his domain and he didn't want any new settlers. But Texas Ranger Jim Branagan had other ideas. Could he put an end to Flint's tyranny for good?

## THE DEVIL RODE A PINTO
### Bret Rey

When a settler is cut to ribbons in a frenzied attack, Texas Ranger Sam Buck learns that the killer is Rufus Berry, known as The Devil. Sam stiffens his resolve to kill or capture Berry and break up his gang.

## THE DEATH MAN
### Lee F. Gregson

The hardest of men went in fear of Ford, the bounty hunter, who had earned the name 'The Death Man'. Yet even Ford was not infallible — when he killed the wrong man, he found that he was being sought himself by the feared Frank Ambler.

## LEAD LANGUAGE
### Gene Tuttle

After Blaze Colton and Ricky Rawlings have delivered a train load of cows from Arizona to San Francisco, they become involved in a load of trouble and find themselves on the run!

## A DOLLAR FROM THE STAGE
### Bill Morrison

Young saddle-tramp Len Finch stumbled into a web of murder, lawlessness, intrigue and evil ambition. In the end, he put his life on the line for the folks that he cared about.

# BRAND 2: HARDCASE
## Neil Hunter

When Ben Wyatt and his gang hold up the bank in Adobe, Wyatt is captured. Judge Rice asks Jason Brand, an ex-U.S. Marshal, to take up the silver star. Wyatt is in the cells, his men close by, and Brand is the only man to get Adobe out of real trouble . . .

# THE GUNMAN AND THE ACTRESS
## Chap O'Keefe

To be paid a heap of money just for protecting a fancy French actress and her troupe of players didn't seem that difficult — but Joshua Dillard hadn't banked on the charms of the actress, and the fact that someone didn't want him even to reach the town . . .

## HE RODE WITH QUANTRILL
### Terry Murphy

Following the break-up of Quantrill's Raiders, both Jesse James and Mel Becher head their own gang. A decade later, their paths cross again when, unknowingly, they plan to rob the same bank — leading to a violent confrontation between Becher and James.


## THE CLOVERLEAF CATTLE COMPANY
### Lauran Paine

Bessie Thomas believed in miracles, and her husband, Jawn Henry, did not. But after finding a murdered settler and his woman, and running down the renegades responsible, Jawn Henry would have time to reflect. He and Bessie had never had children. Miracles evidently did happen.

## COOGAN'S QUEST
### J. P. Weston

Coogan came down from Wyoming on the trail of a man he had vowed to kill — Red Sheene, known as The Butcher. It was the kidnap of Marian De Quincey that gave Coogan his chance — but he was to need help from an unexpected quarter to avoid losing his own life.


## DEATH COMES TO ROCK SPRINGS
### Steven Gray

Jarrod Kilkline is in trouble with the army, the law, and a bounty hunter. Fleeing from capture, he rescues Brian Tyler, who has been left for dead by the three Jackson brothers. But when the Jacksons reappear on the scene, will Jarrod side with them or with the law in the final showdown?